W9-ANW-116

ONE FOOT IN LOVE

~

BY BIL WRIGHT

NEW HANOVER COUNTY
PUBLIC LIBRARY
201 CHESTNUT STREET
WILMINGTON, NC 28401

A TOUCHSTONE BOOK
Published by Simon & Schuster
New York London Toronto Sydney

TOUCHSTONE
Rockefeller Center
1230 Avenue of the Americas
New York, NY 10020

This book is a work of fiction. Names, characters, places, and incidents
either are products of the author's imagination or are used fictitiously.
Any resemblance to actual events or locales or persons, living or dead, is
entirely coincidental.

Copyright © 2004 by Bil Wright
"Tupelo Honey" copyright © 1971 by Van Morrison
All rights reserved, including the right of reproduction in whole or in part
in any form.

TOUCHSTONE and colophon are registered trademarks
of Simon & Schuster Inc.

For information regarding special discounts for bulk purchases,
please contact Simon & Schuster Special Sales at 1-800-456-6798
or business@simonandschuster.com

Designed by Michelle Blau

Manufactured in the United States of America

10 9 8 7 6 5 4 3 2 1

Library of Congress Cataloging-in-Publication Data
Wright, Bil
    One foot in love / by Bil Wright.
        p. cm.
"A Touchstone book."
1. Middle aged women--Fiction. 2. Female friendship--Fiction. 3. Widows--
Fiction. I. Title.
PS3573.R4938O54   2004
813'.54--dc22   2003054464

ISBN 0-7432-4640-3

My sincere thanks to Bill Engel for his continued kindness and generosity.

And to Becket Logan, Cherise Davis, Winifred Golden, Paula West, and my family and friends. God Bless. I am deeply appreciative.

My sincere thanks to Bill Engel for his continued kindness and generosity.

And to Becket Logan, Cherise Davis, Winifred Golden, Paula West, and my family and friends. God Bless. I am deeply appreciative.

Then they returned to Jerusalem from the mount called Olivet, which is near Jerusalem, a Sabbath day's journey away. And when they had entered, they went up to the upper room where they were staying: Peter, James, John, and Andrew; Phillip and Thomas, Bartholomew and Matthew; James the son of Alphaeus and Simon the Zealot; and Judas the son of James. These all continued with one accord in prayer and supplication, *with the women and Mary the mother of Jesus.*

—From the Book of Acts

One

"Mount Olive emergency room. May I help you?"

"Mrs. Terrence Washington, please."

It took her by surprise. No one called her "Mrs. Terrence Washington." And no one ever called Turtle "Terrence."

A mother carrying a tiny young boy rushed up to Rowtina's desk, gasping. "My son—he fell. He was standing on a chair watching me cook. I looked away and before I knew it, he was lying in the middle of the kitchen floor screaming."

Rowtina told her caller to hold on. She paged for immediate transport and an intern. Minutes later, as the child was being whisked away on a gurney, Rowtina picked up the phone again. "May I help you?"

"Mrs. Washington?"

"Yes, that's right."

"This is United Parcel Service. I'm sorry to be making this call, ma'am."

But what the man said to her next—about what had happened to Turtle—didn't make sense. He kept saying how sorry he was.

"You've made a mistake," Rowtina told him, but her breath was short and she had trouble getting it out.

"I'm the dispatcher, ma'am. On your husband's shift. This number is the one he put down in case something should happen to him. It says Rowtina Washington is the person to be called in the event—" The man stopped, then started again. He felt awful about the others, too, he told her. The cashier and the two little boys. The whole thing was a damn shame. "This is the part of my job I wouldn't wish on anybody," he said. "Jesus."

All the colors in the room blurred together. Rowtina held on to the front desk, leaned into it so that the edge cut across her pelvis. She felt like she was melting. "Where is Turtle—where is my husband now?" she asked the dispatcher.

"They took him to St. Theresa's on 173rd Street. To the emergency room." Rowtina knew all about emergency rooms. Sometimes people stayed there for hours—bleeding, having heart attacks, waiting to be paid some attention.

If the dispatcher said something after that, Rowtina didn't remember hearing it. She didn't remember yelling to Dina Tamaris, her shift partner, that she had to leave immediately, there wasn't time to explain. She didn't remember anything except the dispatcher saying how sorry he was with that catch in his voice. Rowtina could still hear him as she ran out into the March night wind. She heard him on the subway up to 168th Street as loud as if he were sitting next to her and behind her and in front of her. "Damn shame. I'm so sorry."

Rowtina knew where St. Theresa's was. She'd passed by it, but neither she nor Turtle had ever had to go there for any reason. She'd made a mental note of where the emergency room entrance was. She always noticed where they were when she passed hospitals now, just as she wondered how other emergency rooms compared to the one she worked in. Tonight she'd find out about St. Theresa's.

It was full, the same as the one downtown at Mount Olive. All kinds of people having a Friday evening medical emergency. Rowtina went directly to the desk and said as calmly as she could, "I got a call that my husband was here. Terrence Washington. I believe he was admitted about an hour ago."

The woman who was doing Rowtina's job in St. Theresa's emergency room asked her to "hold on a minute." She went into a small glass booth where she said something to her own shift partner that Rowtina could've bet had nothing to do with Turtle or any other patient. When she came out again, the woman asked Rowtina, "What was the name you said?"

"Terrence Washington," she told the woman for the second time.

The woman scratched her head with a red pencil. She picked up a clipboard from her desk. Rowtina looked past her, farther down the hall. There were several gurneys lining the walls. "Let me just go in," she wanted to tell the woman. "I'll find him."

The woman called back to her shift partner in the booth. "Hattie, page Dr. Griffin, would ya?" To Rowtina she said, "You need to speak to the head doctor on duty. He'll be out in a minute. You should have a seat."

Rowtina backed away toward the double row of folding chairs. She couldn't have sat even if one of them had been empty. She knew too much about hospital procedure to not understand what was happening. You don't call the doctor out to the waiting area. Not unless . . .

She could hear the dispatcher's voice again. "I can't tell ya how sorry I am."

Dr. Griffin went into the glass booth with Hattie, then out to the woman at the front desk. The woman pointed with her red pencil at Rowtina. The doctor walked toward her in slow motion.

"Mrs. Washington? Could you come this way, please?"

They went into the hallway. *Maybe it's not so bad. Turtle is here and the doctor just wants to tell me what's happened before I see him.*

They passed the emergency room and the doctor asked her to join him in a tiny cell of an office. He gestured toward a dingy yellow plastic chair. Rowtina sat. He stood over her.

"We think your husband may have had a rather severe stroke while he was driving. He lost control of his truck and there was further damage because of injuries sustained to several vital organs." Dr. Griffin sighed and shrugged. "The fact of the matter is there wasn't anything we could do for him here. It was too late. He was already gone."

Gone? Rowtina asked the doctor, "Where is my husband now?"

"We're holding the body in the morgue for identification. I'm very sorry, Mrs. Washington. Can I get you anything?"

Rowtina shook her head no. It was the second stranger tonight who'd told her how sorry he was. She hoped she wouldn't have to hear it again.

Dr. Griffin opened the office door. "Down that way is the East elevator. Get off on 1C. Make a left and go as far as you can. When you get there, give them your husband's name."

Rowtina stood and looked blankly at him. "Thank you," she said. Then she asked herself, *Why? What am I thanking him for? For telling me, "We couldn't do anything for him" ? "He was already gone"?* She started toward the East elevator.

The morgue attendant also had a clipboard with Turtle's name on a list. "Did you come alone?" she asked Rowtina.

"Yes," Rowtina answered. *I'm the one they called. I'm his wife. Who would I have brought with me?*

"Sometimes, it's easier if you have someone else with you. A friend, a relative."

Rowtina thought of her mother. Sylvia Mention was the last person in the world Rowtina would have asked to come with her. Not for this.

"May I see my husband, please?"

"I have to tell you, Mrs. Washington, he was hurt pretty badly. You should prepare yourself."

"Yes," Rowtina said, but she didn't understand how exactly she was supposed to do that. Prepare herself.

The attendant led her into a room that was blindingly bright and cold. She'd been squinting out at the world ever since she'd gotten the call, but she was wild-eyed now, searching around her for Turtle. There were four gleaming silver tables in the center of the room. On them were sheets covering what Rowtina knew were bodies. She recognized Turtle's immediately. All the other shapes seemed too small, but the largest, farthest away from her, was him. She was sure of it.

The attendant motioned with one hand for Rowtina to wait. She went over to one of the tables and lifted the sheet. "It's not Turtle," Rowtina wanted to tell her. "That's not the one. Turtle's over there." The attendant frowned, looked at her clipboard, and put the sheet down. She walked to another table, the table Rowtina knew was the right one. The room seemed to be getting brighter. Rowtina blinked to adjust, watching the attendant lift the sheet again. She looked at Rowtina, then let the sheet fall and stepped forward. Taking Rowtina's arm, she said quietly, "Come, Mrs. Washington." She guided Rowtina to the correct table. When they got there, she asked her, "Are you alright?" Rowtina tried to nod yes, although she wasn't sure her head was moving at all.

The attendant pulled back the sheet, uncovering Turtle. The sheet was so white, and Turtle looked darker than Rowtina had ever seen him. Purplish. Part of his skull was chiseled open. A section of his wide neck, his cheek, and most of his mouth was cut away. *His lips. What happened to his beautiful lips?* Rowtina's hands flew up as if for some specific purpose only they knew, but they stopped in midair just above his face. Rowtina felt the attendant ready to step between her and Turtle. She let her hands fall to her sides again. *Stop. She'll make you leave him here alone again.* Rowtina looked at Turtle's closed eyes. She wanted to open them, for him to be able to see her again. *And I want his mouth back. The way his top lip curls up like he's smiling all the time.*

"That is your husband, isn't it, Mrs. Washington? Terrence G. Washington?" The attendant was eager to check something off on her pad.

"Yes," Rowtina answered. She watched the attendant make her notation.

"Can we step outside, or would you like another few minutes?"

Rowtina wanted the attendant to leave so that she could ask Turtle, "What do you want me to do? Is there anything you want to tell me?" But the attendant wasn't going anywhere, so Rowtina stood for a moment and asked him silently. When the attendant came near her again, Rowtina told Turtle, *She's not going to let us have any time together. I have to go now.*

In the office across the hall, the attendant asked her, "Could you jot down the name and address of the funeral home where you want the body delivered? That's if you know already. If you still need a little time, you could call us in the morning."

Rowtina hadn't come prepared with any names of funeral homes. She hadn't come prepared at all. Her legs had turned gummy and damp. She thought she might have wet herself.

"I'll have to call you tomorrow. I don't know any funeral homes." She started toward the door when the attendant called her back.

"Mrs. Washington, this is for you to take with you." She made it sound like a door prize or a plate of food she was offering because she'd cooked too much and it wouldn't keep. She handed Rowtina a shopping bag with the hospital's name on it. Rowtina opened it. She smelled what was there before she saw it—Turtle's bloody uniform stuffed inside, along with his shoes, socks, and underwear. Rowtina stared at the uniform on top. She put her arms around it and hugged it. *What are we going to do, Turtle? What do you want me to do?*

She went back down the corridor to the East elevator. When she stepped in, someone asked her what floor she wanted, but she didn't say anything. She was still hugging the plastic bag, listening for Turtle's answer. By the time she got home, the smell of his uniform was inside her mouth, the back of her throat. But she held the bag close to her anyway and breathed him in.

Outside their apartment building, she stood looking up at their window on the second floor. *I've got to think of something to do as soon as I get inside. I've got to make a plan so I don't go right back to the hospital and ask can I stay with him, can I be with him in that room.*

She knew she should call her mother immediately because there'd be hell to pay if she didn't. Inside, she sat on their bed and dialed. When her mother answered, Rowtina told her as simply as possible, "Turtle had a stroke, Mama, while he was driving his truck. He lost control and crashed into a supermarket window. Some people in the store were hurt too." Rowtina couldn't make herself say they'd died, and certainly not because of Turtle. "I just came back from St. Theresa's," she said. "From the morgue."

Sylvia Mention was uncharacteristically silent for a moment before responding. "Well, I hope for his sake he died instantly. With something like that, no matter who the person is, I'm sure it's better they be put out of their misery as soon as possible."

Rowtina closed her eyes. "I've got to go now, Mama."

"I know you don't want to think of it that way, but what if he'd lived and been unable to do anything for himself or anybody else? Imagine what your life would have been like then."

"I'm sure it would have been horrible. I really do have to lie down now, Mama. I don't feel very well."

"But when is the funeral, Rowtina?"

"I've got to call the church. I'll let you know when it's settled."

"Did he leave enough to have himself taken care of? Funerals can leave you without a single dollar for the living, you know."

"Yes, Mama, it's all taken care of. I'll be fine. But I've got to hang up now. I told you, I don't feel well."

"You let me know, then," Sylvia Mention answered.

Rowtina heard a click and a dial tone. She hung up the phone and fell back across the bed, still wearing her coat. Quickly she sat up again, took the phone from its cradle, and put it under her pillow. *I can't let you call me back, Mama. There's no way in the world I can let you call me back.*

She spent the night sitting up with the bag containing Turtle's uniform at the foot of the bed. When she glanced at the fluorescent green hands of the clock, they let her know how close to morning it was. At six she got up, achy from sitting so long in the same position. She took the hospital shopping bag off the bed and put it in the corner of the bedroom. Then she called Mount Olive and told Greta Durant, the morning supervisor, that she wouldn't be in for her shift later that afternoon.

"It's the flu," she lied. She didn't say anything about Turtle. Maybe she'd call back when Dina had come on duty and tell her the truth. Dina would certainly start spreading the story. By the time Rowtina went back to work, she wouldn't have to tell anyone anything.

At nine, Rowtina called the Church of Deliverance. It was the church where she and Turtle got married after Sylvia Mention asked their family minister at Jordan Tabernacle to dissuade her daughter from marrying a UPS man. The Church of Deliverance was smaller and neither as grand nor as ceremonious as Jordan Tabernacle, but for Rowtina, it had been a safe haven, a fortress.

In Rowtina's mind, the Church of Deliverance and Reverend Alphonse Otillie, its founding and presiding minister, had ordained her first and only act of defiance against her mother. She'd been a faithful and generous member ever since.

The first year they were married, Rowtina teased Turtle, "You don't have any excuse. Jesus is only blocks away and He's waiting for your behind." But Turtle had told her from the beginning, "I'm not one too much for church." And the one thing he consistently refused her was his presence beside her on Sunday morning, with the exception of one or two Christmas Eve services. Even then he'd asked her, "Why you going to that raggedy little church with no heat and busted-up cushions? You better go on and be religious with some high style like your ma. At least you could pray on Christmas Eve without gettin' your butt frostbit."

At the door to his office, Reverend Otillie took Rowtina's hand in both of his. He asked her to take a seat on his dilapidated office couch. Sitting next to her with a look of gentle concern in his eyes, he cocked his head attentively. Rowtina shifted her weight, trying to avoid the couch's bulging springs under her. She held Turtle's suit in a clothing bag on her lap, hoping it wouldn't wrinkle during their conversation. She was going to take it to whatever funeral home Reverend Otillie recommended.

"You told my secretary your husband had a stroke," Reverend Otillie began. "And yet, was he a fairly young man?"

"Yes. Yes, he was."

Reverend Otillie shook his head, tapped his foot on the worn Oriental carpet. "You're a mighty young woman to be widowed, God bless you."

Rowtina was grateful for this opportunity to tell Reverend Otillie the details. She explained how Turtle's stroke was the reason he'd lost control of his truck—and how she had no way of knowing if her husband was in any pain or if he even knew what was happening to him. Repeating what the dispatcher had said,

Rowtina described the truck going up onto the sidewalk and through the Safeway supermarket window. She told her minister she was praying for the families of the three other innocent people who'd been killed—she hoped God would provide some kind of comfort for the husband of the cashier who'd been struck and for the parents of the two little boys who'd been waiting for her to give them their change.

When Rowtina finished, she was surprised to see Reverend Otillie smiling at her. "You know, Rowtina, about halfway through your story, I realized you attend services here, don't you?"

Rowtina sat up on the edge of the couch. "I've been coming here every Sunday I wasn't working, for eight years. From the time you married Turtle and me." She thought of all the envelopes of money she'd passed his way on Sunday mornings. Many of the Sundays, she'd been the only one in the pew, one out of twelve or thirteen people in the whole church.

Reverend Otillie jumped from the couch as if he'd been stabbed by one of the protruding couch springs and scurried behind his desk. "Our church is enjoying a spirit of divine renewal—every now and then I lose track of somebody. It's only natural. I know you won't hold it against me." He hurried on, "We have a lot going on here this week, but Wednesday seems to be free except for Seniors' Bingo in the social hall. I can schedule an evening service, if you like."

Rowtina stood. Now she was anxious to settle the arrangements and get out of the old man's musty office.

He grinned at her. "You give me your husband's date of birth, surviving family members, years on the job and I'll put something together. Not to worry, Rowtina."

She frowned at him. He was someone who definitely should be calling her "Mrs. Terrence Washington."

"Is there a soloist who could sing 'Blessed Assurance'?" she asked him.

"Sarah Jenkins will sing your husband three quarters of the way to heaven, but it'll add on another hundred dollars to your funeral fee. Sarah Jenkins sang in a show on Broadway starring Miss Ruby Dee. Course there are others I can ask who wouldn't cost as much, it all depends on the quality you're looking for."

Rowtina was more than ready to leave. "Call Sarah Jenkins, please. Do I pay her directly or write the check out to the church?"

"Everything's made payable to the church." Reverend Otillie didn't seem too eager to prolong the meeting either. He was already moving toward the door.

"I didn't give the hospital the name of a funeral home," Rowtina told him. "Who do you usually use?"

Reverend Otillie doubled back to his cluttered desk, reached for a card from a sizable stack, and presented it to Rowtina. "Bailey's. Right here on 156th Street. They do very nice work."

Rowtina brought Turtle's suit to Bailey's Funeral Home. Marion Bailey had a wide, dentured grin and was eager to please. He was equally eager to make sure she signed each of his contract's seven pages.

When he took Turtle's suit from her, he asked about the large pin attached to the lapel.

"It's his UPS Wings of Service medal," Rowtina explained. "I thought he would want to have it on."

She remembered when Turtle had first brought the medal home, along with a certificate, and handed them to her. "Look what they give me," he'd said casually, and had gone into the bedroom to change his clothes.

"It's an award, Turtle! You didn't tell me you were going to get an award!" The Wings of Service certificate said, "Ten Years Without Incident."

Rowtina ran into the bedroom and asked Turtle, "What does 'without incident' mean, honey?"

He'd laughed. "It means I don't drive around with a gut full of gin like some of 'em do and run my truck into the river."

Rowtina didn't share any of this with Bailey. But she did tell him, "It's an important award. He definitely should be wearing it."

For the next four days, Rowtina sat in her apartment, unable to concentrate on anything but what she thought of as Turtle's "accident." She pieced together all of the moments from the time she'd closed the door behind him that morning to the call at the hospital from the dispatcher. She remembered hand-washing two pairs of socks and three pairs of underpants for him after he left because she knew she wouldn't have time to get to the Laundromat before the weekend. She'd brought one of the pairs of underpants and socks to Bailey, the mortician. She didn't know if he'd use them, but she hoped he would. She wanted Turtle to be properly dressed for all of this.

At night, Rowtina couldn't bring herself to lie flat-out in their bed. She sat instead in her place as she had the first night, with her head back against the wall. Sometimes she drifted off for a few minutes, but never too long. She may as well have gone to work, she thought, and been busy, but people would think it was disrespectful and wonder if she'd really cared about him.

There was no way to avoid her mother's calls. All she could do was try to keep the conversations as brief as possible. She assured Sylvia Mention she didn't need anything to eat or drink, to be shopped for or visited. When her mother called on Tuesday morning to ask if she had a dress for the funeral, she made the mistake of telling her, "Turtle always told me if something happened to him not to wear black, so I think I'll wear a dress he really liked to see me in."

Sylvia Mention snorted. "Don't let your grief make you embarrass yourself."

Rowtina promised, "I won't, Mama," but now she worried that the dark green dress Turtle had said made her look like a sexy willow tree would do exactly what her mother warned her against.

Later that morning, she kept her appointment to go back to Bailey's Funeral Home to approve what Marion Bailey had done to Turtle.

Bailey, with the same horsy grin, led Rowtina to a closed door with the number 3 in gold metal nailed onto the outside. "Now I want you to keep in mind if you will," he told her, "that we had our work cut out for us. I believe we did the very best we could. I hope you'll be pleased."

She had barely stepped inside the room when she realized what Bailey had been trying to explain. Without actually going anywhere near the casket, she could see that the "very best" Marion Bailey could do wasn't good enough. The copper color in Turtle's cheeks and forehead had apparently been erased permanently. He wasn't even purple anymore. Just gray, ashen. The widow's peak of tight black curls that made him look like a mischievous eleven year old had been erased by the accident. Anyone who wanted to see it again would have to summon it from memory. Rowtina didn't want to get any closer to see what Marion Bailey had substituted for the parts of Turtle's face that had been torn away. She turned and left the room.

"As I tried to tell you—" the mortician began.

"I know," Rowtina stopped him.

"Well, then, what is your decision about the viewing?" He was indignant, offended. He managed to close his thin lips in a stretched-out grimace over his ill-fitting false teeth.

"There won't be one," Rowtina told him.

That night, she sat on the bed and stared at the bag she'd brought from the hospital with Turtle's clothes in it. She thought about what she'd seen from a distance at the funeral home. *You were handsome, Turtle. I know how handsome you were.*

She closed her eyes, remembering how she'd chased Turtle's truck through a snowstorm the day she'd met him—waving the "Final Attempt to Deliver" slip he'd left on the front door. It was Sylvia Mention who thought she heard the buzzer, then glanced out the window to see him driving away. "See if you can catch that man, Rowtina," her mother told her.

By the time he stopped for a red light, Rowtina was so out of breath, she couldn't do anything but hold up the slip of paper. He looked down at her from his seat on the truck and laughed. "This is the first time I had a woman chase down my truck before. And a fine somethin' of a woman at that. Shoooooeeee!"

Rowtina thought it was just the kind of line a man who looked like him would use, with his big chest and hazel eyes. When he said his name was Turtle, though, she shocked herself by telling him, "Now you're lying. That's nobody's real name."

"It's mine," he insisted, laughing. Turned out Rowtina was right—he was lying, although that's not what he called it.

It was almost another month before she knew the truth. "How can I introduce my mother to somebody named Turtle?" she teased him, not realizing she had a choice. Turtle pulled out his driver's license and showed it to her. "I'm Turtle to you," he said. "And your mother, too, if you think me and her'll hit it off. If not, you can introduce me as Terrence G. Washington."

Rowtina tried to be angry at the deception, but Turtle shrugged and said, "If I'd told you my name was Terrence G. Washington, you woulda thought I made it up just to impress ya." As it turned out, Sylvia Mention hardly referred to Turtle by any name at all for as long as she knew him. It was only after they were married that she stopped calling him "the UPS man."

*　*　*

At the funeral, Sylvia Mention sat in the first row, next to her daughter. Rowtina could feel her mother's disapproval at her wearing the green dress Turtle liked her in so much. Sylvia Mention had glared so sourly at it when she walked up to Rowtina at the church, Rowtina had almost decided to keep her coat on for the service, but it would have been too hot. *Besides,* she reminded herself, *I wore this for Turtle, not for Mama.*

Rowtina suspected Sylvia Mention might have changed her mind about sitting in the front row altogether had she realized she'd be sitting next to Turtle's three brothers, Hubie, B. J., and Rap. Minutes after she'd first met them at Rowtina's wedding reception, she'd called them "the Flintstone boys." They were big and loud, but also friendly and courteous, Rowtina thought. She understood there wasn't anything they could have done to gain her mother's approval other than to disappear altogether, making sure to take their brother with them.

Sylvia inched away from her son-in-law's brothers in the first row as much as she could, pinning her daughter into the corner of the pew. She spread her coat around her as if it were a barrier that could keep them from getting any closer. Rowtina turned quickly to glance around the church. She hadn't really expected anyone except Turtle's brothers and her mother. Turtle's dispatcher had called to find out the address of the church, and Rowtina knew Turtle had several buddies from the job, but she didn't know if any of them would actually attend his service. There was a small knot of them, though, enough to fill one of the small pews. Rowtina nodded shyly in their direction. *I've got to remind myself to send them a thank-you card.*

There also appeared to be two women behind the row of men, but Rowtina couldn't see who they were. Probably the couple of women drivers Turtle had mentioned. He'd told her how the men gave them such a rough time.

Rowtina knew it was odd not to have friends of her own there.

She'd received a card from Dina and several other members of the emergency room staff, but she certainly didn't expect to see them at the church. How many times had Turtle cautioned her, "You got to find something else to fill up your life besides church and Old Slow Turtle. Get yourself on a bowling league or learn how to play cards." But Rowtina had felt so lucky to have Turtle. If there'd been a baby, it might have been different. But from the time they knew there wasn't going to be any baby—there couldn't be—she only felt closer to Turtle. Sitting across the dinner table from him or even waiting for him to get there was a hundred times better than any bowling league. When he wasn't home, she simply read the romance novels she bought with her discount at the hospital gift shop.

Rowtina closed her eyes. Sarah Jenkins began the "Blessed Assurance" she'd paid an extra hundred dollars for in a wobbly, swooping soprano. It must've been a long time since Sarah Jenkins had been on Broadway.

Rowtina remembered how astonished she'd been to hear Turtle singing it one night from the bathtub, about a month after they were married. "I thought you weren't a religious man," she'd laughed. "I'm not a churchgoing man," he'd answered. "That don't make me a heathen. I can sing a hymn if I want to, can't I?" Blessed Assurance was exactly what she was looking for now. She'd hoped it would come from old Reverend Otillie, but that clearly was a mistake on her part.

When the song was over, Reverend Otillie began to deliver Turtle's eulogy. He sounded like a weatherman his first time on air, jabbering about seasonal temperatures with no significant changes for the next three days.

Somewhere inside Rowtina an alarm went off. She felt she had to ask Turtle if she'd done what it was he wanted her to with all of this. She called out to him, "Did I, Turtle?" She closed her eyes to concentrate, because old man Otillie was going on with some real nonsense about parting with loved ones. Rowtina had no intention of parting with anyone. She called again louder, "Did I do what you wanted me to, Turtle?!" When Otillie started shouting that Terrence Washington's family and friends should be happy he'd found a better place to live than this old troubled earth, Rowtina blurted so that she didn't have to hear him at all, "I really am sorry, Turtle. But I couldn't think of anything else to do!"

When she opened her eyes, B. J. had his arm around her, rocking her from side to side, telling her, "Turtle hears you, alright. He's not wantin' any apologies from you." Sylvia Mention was looking at her as if she didn't recognize her, as if Rowtina were a total stranger, the uncouth girlfriend of one of these over-grown idiots she had to share a pew with—but not her daughter.

Someone else put her hands on Rowtina's neck from behind. Warm, firm. Right at the base of her skull, as though keeping it in place. Rowtina turned to see a woman's face lowering to meet hers. It was a nurse from Mount Olive, the one Rowtina had heard Izzie the custodian speak so rudely about one night when she was leaving.

The nurse whispered into her ear. "I'm Nelda Battey from Six North at Mount Olive. Here's a little support for ya."

Nelda leaned over and took Rowtina's hands. She clasped them around a linen napkin, which contained something hard and smooth, but she couldn't tell what. Sylvia Mention looked from Rowtina's lap, where this sleight of hand was going on, up to Nelda Battey, as though she were about to ask Nelda what exactly she thought she was doing. But the nurse had already gone back to her seat.

Reverend Otillie invited the congregation to stand and sing the hymn "Farther Along." Sylvia pounced on Rowtina. "Who the hell was that?"

"She's a nurse at Mount Olive."

Rowtina looked back again and saw that Nelda Battey was one of the two women she'd seen in the row behind Turtle's UPS buddies. Standing next to her, singing, was another woman she recognized from the hospital, an aide about her mother's age. The older woman continued to sing as she smiled at Rowtina and nodded. *I don't know either one of them. What are they doing here?*

Sylvia Mention nudged her daughter. "What did she give you?"

"I don't know, I . . ." Rowtina unwrapped the linen napkin to find a shiny, gold flask with the initials N.A.B. engraved on it.

"Good Lord!" Sylvia Mention muttered.

B. J. Washington, sitting next to Sylvia, called out, "Whatcha got there, Rowtina?" and the other two brothers leaned over to see for themselves.

Rowtina tried to hide the flask, but Sylvia Mention pushed so hard against her, trying to get away from B. J., that it slipped out of Rowtina's hand to the floor. Rowtina leaned over to retrieve it. Her mother hissed, "Don't touch it." Rowtina froze, mid-lean.

B. J. assured them, "I got it." He fell to his knees, reached across Sylvia's ankles as she focused solemnly on the casket, and grabbed the flask.

On his way back up, Sylvia whispered through her teeth, "Keep it."

B. J. nodded. "Yes ma'am, I will," but he winked some message at Rowtina that she didn't understand.

When the funeral was over, a few of the UPS men came up to Rowtina. One of them who smelled like he might have had a few drinks said, "I hope you know how crazy he was about you." The rest of them shook her hand and mumbled about what an alright guy Turtle was. Nelda Battey and the other woman from Mount Olive seemed to have disappeared. *I'll get cards for both of them,* Rowtina thought. *And I'll write a special note.*

Rowtina and Sylvia Mention rode to the cemetery in B. J.'s car, following the hearse. Hubie and Rap were behind them. Rowtina was grateful to be driven by B. J., particularly since it meant that Sylvia would be silent as long as he was in the car with them. As they drove through Longacre Memorial Park, Rowtina gazed around her. She was forty years old and had never been in a cemetery before. *I don't want to leave him here,* she thought. *It's not even pretty.*

At the grave site, Rowtina stared up at the overcast sky rather than look at the casket again. Reverend Otillie led her and the four others in the Lord's Prayer. Then he began the Twenty-third Psalm. Rowtina had heard it hundreds of times since she was growing up. But when Reverend Otillie got to, "Yea, though I walk through the valley of the shadow of death, I will fear no evil," she realized she'd never considered what the valley of the shadow of death might really be. She thought about Turtle's truck crashing through the window of the supermarket with him in the driver's seat. No one had been able to tell her for sure if he was still alive then or not. *He was there—in the valley of the shadow of death. Was he afraid?*

She remembered how he'd looked on the metal table at St. Theresa's morgue and again in the casket at Bailey's Funeral Home. Everything she'd loved about his face was gone. Death had been cruel, frighteningly cruel. Had she been afraid? Yes. And now she was afraid again—to leave Turtle here in this hole in the ground, in this ugly plot of dirt. *I will fear no evil,* she told herself. *I will fear. No evil.*

As B. J. escorted Rowtina back to the car, she felt him slip the flask into her coat pocket. Reverend Otillie walked up to her and said, "Don't you be a stranger now. This is the time to stay close to your church home and renew your faith." *'Blessed Assurance,'* Rowtina thought. *He ought to take that off my bill.*

Once Sylvia Mention realized Rowtina was not inviting Turtle's brothers back to the apartment, she insisted on coming herself. "We should talk about what you're going to do now."

As soon as they got inside, Mrs. Mention instructed Rowtina, "Lay out all your financial papers on the bed. That way we can see what you need to worry about."

Rowtina held her tongue and went directly into the bath-room. She locked the door, slammed the toilet seat lid down, and sat with her fingers in her ears as she'd done when she was seven. She hummed and tapped her foot—she'd called it the Drowning-Out Song when she was a girl—but it was as useless now as it had always been. The sound of Sylvia Mention could not be diminished. "If you tell me where everything is"—her voice rang out like a drill piercing the bathroom wall—"I'll start to sort it out for you. It shouldn't take long, if you've been orga-nized at all."

Rowtina stayed inside until she assumed her mother had wearied of talking to the bathroom door. When she went out, though, she understood why her mother had given up her one-sided conversation about Rowtina's finances. Sylvia Mention had found a project she didn't need her daughter's help with. From the dresser Rowtina and Turtle shared, her mother had emptied Turtle's clothes onto the bed and was busy stuffing them into plastic garbage bags.

"Do you have any more of these?" Mrs. Mention held up one of the bags. "I've used up what was left in the box I found under the sink." When Rowtina didn't answer immediately, Mrs. Men-tion went back to her task. "Most of it can go to Goodwill," she said. "I left the uniforms separate. Maybe you can call UPS and have somebody come get them. Some other driver would proba-bly be glad to have them."

Rowtina leapt toward her. "You have to stop, Mama. We can't do this."

"*You* can't, honey, and I understand. That's why I'm doing it for you."

"No. Stop. You have to stop!" It was almost a yell. Near

enough, certainly, for Sylvia Mention to look up sharply into her daughter's face. If Rowtina had been ten or even fifteen, she might have been slapped for her insolence. But when her mother's eyes met hers, Rowtina was sure Sylvia Mention saw something that surprised her. She stared in the same way she had when Rowtina began to call out questions to Turtle in church. She must have seen the lines in Rowtina's forehead and the way her jaw kept moving back and forth involuntarily like it had come loose from the rest of her face. Sylvia Mention must have decided that there was something so unfamiliar, so unnatural about her daughter in that moment that it was obvious she was beyond reason. She watched silently as Rowtina undid the knots she'd tied so meticulously at the mouth of each bag. Pulling out all of the clothes, Rowtina padded back and forth to the dresser with them, placing them back into it as though she'd just washed and ironed them fresh for Turtle.

Softly, Sylvia Mention said to her daughter, "If now is not the right time for us to begin to get things in order, I suppose it can wait until you're feeling better. When are you planning on going back to work?"

Rowtina answered from her knees, where she was refolding one of Turtle's favorite shirts—a green and yellow plaid. "Monday," she said. "They asked me if I wanted to take some more time, but I said no."

Sylvia Mention reached for her coat. "Good. It's probably better that way." She stood for a moment, waiting. When Rowtina didn't move, Sylvia went to her. She leaned down so that Rowtina could lift her face for a kiss good-bye. Rowtina felt her there but didn't look up. She continued to stroke the collar of a burgundy sweater Turtle wore on cold days over his UPS shirt. Sylvia bent further and kissed the top of her daughter's head. "Come to my church, Sunday morning. I'll make an early dinner for later."

When her mother was gone, Rowtina sat back on the floor in

front of the open dresser drawer. She stared at the shirts and sweaters, socks and underwear, picturing Turtle in them all, until the room was dark around her. It was then that she remembered one more bag of his things, one that her mother had not noticed—thank God—over in the corner on the floor of the bedroom. It was the bag the morgue attendant had given her. She went over and sat on the floor next to it.

Rowtina could barely get control of her trembling hands as she pulled the uniform out of the bag for the first time. She knew already that there was blood, but she hadn't thought there would be so much. She choked on the stench of it mixed with the odor of Turtle's sweat and the picture she had of strangers stripping his uniform off him with rubber gloves—leaving him naked on the silver metal table in St. Theresa's morgue.

She folded it again, placed it back in the bag, and folded the top over twice.

I'll wash this tomorrow. And I'll put it in the drawer with the rest.

She stood and went back to their bed. It had been nearly a week since she'd actually slept in it. Staring at Turtle's side, she thought, *Is this the empty that's supposed to look like he'll never sleep here again? Why does it look the same as the empty that says he'll be coming through the door in an hour or two, as soon as he gets home from driving the late shift? There isn't any difference at all.*

Sleeping next to, on top of, or under Turtle was one of Rowtina's favorite parts of being married to him. Whether they made love, sang old songs by the Four Tops or the Temptations, or held hands until they drifted off, she liked to pretend that sleep married them anew each time they lay down with each other. Turtle's favorite position was to sleep with his hand on her belly or between her thighs. One foot would roam up and down her leg until it found a comfortable place to rest. Rowtina would tease him, "Turtle Washington, if you wanna keep rubbin' up against me while I'm trying to get my rest, you'll get up and put some lotion on that old foot of yours. You're about to bruise my leg with that old tough foot." Turtle would chuckle and whisper into her ear, "Hush. I got one foot in love. And love is gonna soften that old tough foot up—tenderize it, baby. Make the other foot jealous it couldn't find no sweet leg to lay on for itself."

Then he'd chuckle, ease his hand a little higher from her belly to between her breasts, and nuzzle the part of her arm that was a half shade lighter than the rest of her. Soon he'd be snoring softly with a half hum and Rowtina would drift off a few minutes later, smiling. It didn't really matter what Turtle's feet felt like— rough and calloused or soft and damp, fresh from his bath—as long as one of them was there, resting on her calf.

I've got to try to sleep tonight, by myself. She went to her purse and pulled out Nelda Battey's flask. She still couldn't imagine what Nelda and that other woman were doing at Turtle's service in the first place.

Rowtina unscrewed the top and sniffed. "My God!" She closed her eyes tight, took a small sip, swallowed, and followed that immediately with a generous swig. Thumping her chest, she tap danced in place. Once she'd recovered, she turned the flask up again, only slightly this time, shimmied the heat around in her mouth, forward and back. *I shouldn't be doing this. I've got no tolerance for liquor. Never did. None whatsoever.* She announced to the empty apartment, "I've got to go to bed. That's what I've got to do."

Warmed by whiskey, Rowtina unzipped her dress and stepped out of it. She wobbled as she took off her stockings, balancing on one foot and then the other. *I'm gonna sleep naked tonight. Turtle likes it when I sleep naked.*

She pulled her panties down, but she was unable to step out of them for a moment. She wore the same shy blush as on her wedding night. That night, Turtle had caught her from behind, flicked the small of her back right down to her buttocks with his tongue. "I might have to keep you awake all night long, Rowtina Washington." At thirty two years old, she'd never slept in a bed with anyone but her mother, and she absolutely wasn't used to any of what her mother called "sex talk." But the things Turtle said didn't make her feel at all like Sylvia Mention said they would.

She slid onto her side of the bed, leaving Turtle's as undisturbed as possible. Curled like a crescent moon, looking off the edge, she was slow to stretch out the full length of her body. She slid one leg back toward where he'd been with her every night for eight years.

It wasn't really Turtle on that metal tray, smashed and broken. She'd lied at the morgue when she'd said it was her husband she was looking at. No certificate of death with the city's seal on it could make her believe it was Turtle she'd left in Brooklyn lying in a big ugly hole in the ground. Rowtina rolled over onto her back and swept her hand against the clean sheets stretched tight to the other side. Tonight, she was going to look up from their bed and see the real Turtle, think how she couldn't wait to feel all of him, as much as she could grab hold of, with as many parts of her as could take him in. And he'd be whole. No wounds, no bruises, no broken teeth or crushed bones. He'd be big and thick brown and some extra besides. She'd hear him grin when she finally let go of him, stretched her hands out to the walls, then around him again. Pinching, slapping his shoulders, his long, wide back down to his basketball butt. They'd laugh at how good they were together.

"Turtle," she whispered. "I want you to tell me you haven't gone anywhere, that you're still here."

She eased herself further down into the bed on her side, concentrating. *Show me. Please, Turtle. Show me.* She'd whispered these exact words on their first night together in this bed. Now, eight years later, she was asking him again. *Show me.*

Could she? Yes, she could. She could feel Turtle's hard, truck driver's foot on her ankle, then up and down her calf, as always. She was certain of it. "I got one foot in love. It's gonna soften up all by itself and make the other foot jealous it couldn't find no sweet leg to lay on for itself."

Rowtina held her breath.

I should give myself a test, pick out the shapes in the room I know to see if I'm drunk off that whiskey in the flask. Alright. There's the dresser. And the plant on the windowsill. I am in our apartment on 146th Street in Harlem, New York. I am not drunk. This doesn't have a thing to do with that whiskey.

My God, Turtle. Maybe it's a miracle, maybe it's not. But you're here.

She couldn't actually see him, and she was too astonished, too grateful to try to have a conversation with him. But she did feel Turtle's foot move up and down her calf, then stop, resting heavy and warm as it had ever been. Rowtina lay as still as she could and waited. After several minutes, neither of them had spoken or moved. Rowtina told herself, *If he just wants to be here with me, quiet and peaceful, I should respect that.*

One, then two, then several hours passed. Turtle's foot was still there, Rowtina was certain. And she was also certain when—without any warning—she felt him lift himself from her. Still, she couldn't bring herself to move right away.

"Turtle?" she whispered, but she knew he wasn't there anymore. Turtle was gone. Again.

Two

Each night for the next three weeks, she bathed and oiled herself, making herself ready for him in case he came again. He'd told her once, "You feel smoother than any woman I've known." She wanted him to know she was doing her best to keep herself that way for him.

When she went back to Mount Olive that Monday, employees around the hospital seemed genuinely concerned about her. A few stopped by the emergency room desk to express their condolences and welcome her back. Dina Tamaris, who'd become a widow two years before, told her, "I'm the one person you don't have to explain to what you're going through. I know exactly what it's like." Rowtina thought how far that was from the truth.

She had very little appetite, but was full of nervous energy, anticipating when the next night with Turtle might be. Each morning, she awoke tired and disappointed. She made notes on a calendar she kept on her dresser. "No Turtle last night, maybe tonight," and "Thought for sure he'd come this week. Couldn't say why exactly. Just thought he would." For days, all she thought about at the emergency room desk was getting home to wait for Turtle. Each night, she was filled with the same sense of hope.

Exactly a month later, on a drizzly Saturday evening at half past eleven, Rowtina was sitting on the edge of their bed lotion-

ing the insides of her thighs when it occurred to her she was
being watched.

She lifted her legs, eased herself onto the bed as slowly as
possible, and waited. She didn't move, lest she do anything too
suddenly and startle him. Hours passed. Finally, Rowtina was
certain she felt Turtle's foot on her calf. More than that, she
thought—no, she knew—she heard him sigh as though he were
about to tell her something. "What is it, Turtle? Tell me. Go on,
tell me. Please."

But as still as she held herself listening, he said nothing. In
less time than he'd spent with her the time before, he was gone.

The next afternoon, moping listlessly through her shift, she
got a call from the sixth floor nurses' station.

"Rowtina? It's Nelda Battey. Remember? From your husband's service? I passed you the smelling salts."

*Smelling salts? Is she trying to be funny? She was the one with
the flask.*

"Of course, I remember. You were very kind. I'm sorry I
haven't returned your, uh . . . to you."

"Take your time. I don't need it. That's not why I'm calling. I
want to get together with you for dinner one night this week."

Rowtina hesitated. "I hardly ever take my whole dinner
break."

"But you could, couldn't you? We're on the same shift. What
about tomorrow night? Is seven too late for you?"

"No," Rowtina told the sixth floor head nurse weakly. She
didn't understand what the woman could want. "I could meet you
at seven. Seven is good."

"Do you want to go out, or should we rough it in the cafeteria?"

"We could rough it, I suppose." Although she hated the way it
sounded. Rowtina was feeling more uncomfortable by the second. Still, she decided, it was better to stay in the hospital, where
she could excuse herself easily.

"Tomorrow at seven, then." Nelda Battey hung up without saying good-bye.

Rowtina was especially careful around the other black women in the hospital. She had worked hard not to let her own shyness be misconstrued for standoffishness or worse, as she'd been accused of on other jobs. Sylvia Mention taught her early on, "Once you got a whole building of black women against you, you may as well fold your tent. They're the only women in the world who can make turning their backs on you feel worse than if they'd knocked you down and walked over you in six-inch pumps." But Rowtina knew this first-hand because she'd been thought of as snobbish by her coworkers at the nursing home, which was the job before Mount Olive. She'd finally left because it was too hard trying to work with people not speaking to you because they thought you weren't speaking to them.

Rowtina remembered what she'd heard Izzy, the night custodian, profess to three other janitors about Nurse Nelda Battey. They were walking out ahead of Rowtina and had seen Nurse Battey in the distance. "You have yourself a good night, Nurse," Izzie called out. Then he'd turned to his buddies. "That there's a woman-lovin' woman if I ever saw one. Not a thing we got that woman thinks she could use. But I bet if I had about two minutes with her in the broom closet, she'd come out singin' a different tune." The other janitors snickered until they realized Rowtina was behind them. "Night, night, Mrs. Washington." Izzie turned and grinned. Rowtina hadn't responded. It wasn't even what he'd said about Nelda Battey as much as the savage contempt in his voice that frightened and disgusted her.

The next night, Rowtina left the emergency room for her dinner break at five minutes till seven. Sylvia Mention had instilled upon her, "Lateness means you don't give a damn. It's a sure sign of utter disrespect."

Rushing into the cafeteria, she knew within seconds that Nelda was not there yet. She bought a piece of blueberry pie and a cup of tea. Then she picked out a table where no one else was sitting. It was also near one of the exits. This way, it would be easier to leave quickly.

Nelda Battey strode into the cafeteria at seven-fifteen. She waved briskly to the men behind the counter and to Bernice, the cashier, but it was clear she was searching the room. Rowtina waved to her meekly from her table. Nelda rushed over. "Sorry. I should have warned you. I don't ever leave for a break on time. I can plan all I want, but the minute I'm ready to leave, there's a crisis."

Rowtina told her, "I understand. I just got here myself." She was a little overwhelmed by Nelda's energy. It was as though a strong wind had come in through the cafeteria doorway and blown directly on her. Nelda nodded toward Rowtina's pie. "I thought we were gonna have dinner. I'm not that late, am I?"

Rowtina smiled shyly. "No, it's me. I'm not that hungry."

Nelda quipped, "Well, this girl's got to eat more than blueberries and crust. I'll be right back."

Rowtina picked at her pie as she watched Nelda move along the counter, ordering her food. She came back with a tray heaped with pot roast, mashed potatoes, salad, and a plump, buttered biscuit. Before she'd even sat down she began, "I've seen you once or twice since the funeral, coming in or leaving. I didn't get a chance to say anything, you were moving so fast."

"I should have come upstairs to thank you. And to return this." Rowtina reached into her bag and pulled out Nelda's flask. She'd rinsed it out with dish-washing detergent and put it in a small Macy's shopping bag with two rubber bands around it so that no one could see what was inside.

Nelda glanced at the bag quizzically, then put it on the table. Rowtina wished she'd put it out of sight.

"How are you doing?"

"Oh"—Rowtina looked around the room, embarrassed by the bag with the flask in it—"I'm fine. Really fine."

"Well, since I barely know you I may not be the best judge"—Nelda kept her voice low—"but you don't look so 'really fine.'"

Rowtina pulled away. Nelda was right. She barely knew her, so why was she insulting her? She was about to excuse herself from the table when Nelda said, "Don't take it personally. I'm only thinking it would be a damn miracle if you just buried your husband and were feeling so 'really fine' this soon afterward. But hell, if you are, you are. Look, the reason I wanted to have dinner was to invite you to a meeting," the nurse told her.

"What kind of meeting?" Rowtina wished she hadn't thought of Izzie and the janitors at that moment, but she did.

"It's a group I belong to. There aren't that many of us. Not that we're trying to be so selective, but we're not putting any ads in the papers either."

"What kind of group is it, exactly?" Rowtina didn't want to offend Nelda, but she was preparing to straighten her out if Nelda had made any wrong assumptions about her.

"It's a women's group. We meet right here in the hospital. My friend, Osceola McQueen—she was with me at your husband's service—it was her idea."

"But what made her get the idea to start a women's group? What was the purpose?"

Nelda answered, "She started the group in memory of her daughter, Kara."

"In memory?" Rowtina frowned. "Your group isn't especially for women who are in mourning, is it? Because I don't think I need anything like that."

"It's not about mourning at all," Nelda said crisply. "You should come to the next meeting. You'll see. Actually, we'll be celebrating Kara's birthday at the beginning. She would've been thirty-two this year. Then we'll get on with business."

"What's the business?"

"Come next week and find out. What have you got to lose? If you don't want to come back, we can still be friends and I'll never bring it up again."

Rowtina had a last bite of pie, took a sip of tea. "Well, I thank you for letting me know about it. I'll think about it. I will. But I should get back to work now. We're really busy tonight."

"I'll call downstairs and remind you. Believe me, I'm not a club kinda woman myself. So I understand if you have reservations."

Rowtina stood and picked up her tray. "Nelda, you never told me what the name of the group is."

Nelda smiled. "It's called Leave Him and Live."

Rowtina frowned. "I don't understand."

"No reason you should." Nelda chewed a forkful of pot roast and pushed a pair of expensive looking tortoise-shell sunglasses further up onto her forehead. "But do yourself a favor, would you, and come by."

Rowtina nodded. She repeated the name of the group to herself as she took the elevator back downstairs and took her place behind the desk. *Leave Him and Live. What's that got to do with me? I don't need to leave anybody. I'm the one who's been left.*

She stared up at the clock. Four hours to go. She'd already decided she'd sleep naked again tonight. With a little cologne on certain parts of her body.

When Nelda called her again the next week, Rowtina agreed to go to a meeting because she thought it might take her mind off waiting. Waiting and being disappointed. Going meant taking an early dinner break, which wasn't a problem, except that it made the hours before she went home seem even longer. She took the elevator to the room on the seventh floor off Mount Olive's chapel where Nelda said they met. Rowtina entered through the chapel and stopped to look at a stained glass window of Jesus. Her mother would say if Turtle was lucky, he was with Jesus. That meant Jesus was probably making the decisions about whether he came back to her or not. Rowtina silently prayed, "Could you please allow Turtle to come? I'd be very grateful. Amen." She crossed herself even though she wasn't Catholic. She thought it would help seal the prayer.

Osceola McQueen greeted Rowtina at the door. Rowtina recognized her immediately as the other woman who'd been with Nelda at Turtle's funeral. Now that she had a closer look, Rowtina decided Osceola was probably in her mid-sixties. She had sparse, badly dyed hair, the color of cranberries, with silver threads running through it. Osceola was a nurse's aide, Rowtina had found out, who worked mostly on the eighth floor in the Critical Care unit. She hugged Rowtina and told her, "We're so happy to have you here." Rowtina flinched, but smiled and whispered, "Thank you, ma'am. I meant to send you a card to express my appreciation for you coming to my husband's service. I've been so distracted lately. I apologize."

Nelda came in and walked directly over to Rowtina and Osceola. "I was gonna go right downstairs to the emergency room and get your butt if you hadn't shown up voluntarily." Rowtina smiled nervously. She still didn't feel all that comfortable with Nelda. She wasn't sure if she even liked her.

Nelda introduced Rowtina to a huge woman wearing a faded gold and brown waitress's uniform. She had stringy blonde hair with lots of gray in it. When the woman grinned, Rowtina saw that several of her front teeth were missing. She licked what appeared to be a smudge of jam and toast crumbs from her fingers. "Hi, I'm Lucy Antiglione," she said, extending her hand to

Rowtina. "I work downstairs at the Buttered Bun, the coffee shop right next to the hospital." She gestured toward Osceola and Nelda. "That's where those two picked me up."

Rowtina knew she had no choice but to place her hand against Lucy's palm as quickly as she could, avoiding the fingers shiny with saliva. She turned to Nelda. "Is this the whole group?"

"We got one more coming," Lucy rasped in a voice that sounded like she smoked at least a pack of cigarettes a day. She said to Osceola and Nelda, "Egyptia was on the first floor in a phone booth when I came in. Said to tell y'all she'd be up in a second."

Nelda explained, "Egyptia's a teacher uptown. She gets here as soon as she can from school."

Rowtina hadn't thought there'd be so few members. She looked at the circle of five chairs in the middle of the room. She was hoping she'd be able to sit in the back and sneak out after the meeting began.

"I'm here!" A tiny woman impeccably dressed in a cherry-red wool suit with matching dyed pumps rushed in by way of the chapel. "Sorry to be late, but it was important. You'll understand when I explain later on."

Osceola introduced Rowtina to Egyptia, who gave her a rather obvious once-over before allowing, "Nice to meet you, Rowena." She was already on her way to her seat when she said it. No one, including Rowtina, bothered to correct her. Nelda, Lucy, Egyptia, and Rowtina took their seats. Osceola stood in front of them with her hands folded in front of her like a choir soloist.

"Sisters," she affirmed. "Kara McQueen would have been thirty-two years old today. Besides being my daughter, she was a young woman of integrity and honor and a loving person. One of the things that pleased her most was having a big fuss made over her birthday." Osceola smiled impishly. "So I've been baking like a crazy woman and I brought us some refreshments for later I know she would have enjoyed." Rowtina saw the smile leave Osceola's face and her chest begin to rise and fall so quickly that it scared her. "Kara is the person I admired most in this world. Kara . . . is still my hero."

As the women applauded, Rowtina noticed that Nelda had one hand over her mouth and her eyes were almost closed.

"Now," Osceola continued, "for the first order of business, I want to officially welcome Rowtina Washington." She began to applaud. Rowtina could not have been more embarrassed at having four women she didn't know clapping in her direction. Fortunately, Osceola cut them off by continuing, "Now I'm going to turn the meeting over to Lucy. I believe she's got some news."

"Hiya, Sisters!" Lucy stood and immediately began to rock from side to side, smoothing her snug gold uniform over her belly. She grinned so that now Rowtina was fairly certain Lucy had no front teeth at all. "I got a progress report for y'all."

Osceola clapped encouragingly. Lucy continued, "I'm happy to report I've moved to my sister's in Staten Island and I'm pressing assault charges against the pimple-assed bastard known as Salvatore Antiglione."

Osceola, Nelda, and Egyptia yelled so loudly, Rowtina looked to the door to make sure it was closed. She smiled at Lucy to let her know she had her support also, even though she could only guess at the full meaning of Lucy's announcement. Lucy threw her hammy fists into the air to let the Sisters know she hadn't finished. "And, with Egyptia's help, I found a dentist who will fix me up with a porcelain partial on a six-payment plan!"

This time, the three other women jumped to their feet, laughing and hooting as Lucy saucily pointed to her toothless gums. Rowtina stood also and couldn't help but chuckle. Lucy went on. "If the weasel comes within an inch of me or my new teeth, I swear I'll mow him down like a patch of friggin' crabgrass."

Egyptia and Osceola hugged her, while Nelda looked across at Rowtina. Rowtina nodded to signal that it was all very impressive, and it truly was, she thought, but she still didn't know why Nelda felt it had anything to do with her.

"I believe Egyptia has the second order of business. Is that right Egyptia?"

"Thank you, Osceola." Egyptia stood and smoothed the front of her skirt. "The reason I was a little tardy is that I was making sure this was an appropriate time to share my news. As you know, Sisters, after my own divorce I've had six or seven false starts with different gentlemen. And, as you also know, I'm not one for casual dalliances."

Lucy hooted. "I wish to hell I had a piece o' ass to have a 'dalliance' with. Sounds pretty damn good to me."

"Shhhh!" reprimanded Osceola. "Let Egyptia have her turn, Lucy!"

Lucy answered, "Sorry, so sorry," and Egyptia continued.

"I'm here to testify that my losing streak is over. I want to announce my engagement to Mr. Luther Wooldridge. The man's got everything I've prayed for." She paused for a second, and then said in a pitiful Mae West imitation, "With an extra big bonus thrown in besides."

Lucy especially enjoyed this. She hooted, coughed her cigarette cough, and slapped her thighs. Osceola beamed as though Egyptia were graduating from college. Nelda called out, "Alright Miss Egyptia with your Bonus Man!"

"This is it, Sisters," Egyptia cooed. "I'm sure of it. I'm gonna be a Mrs. again."

Once again, the Sisters were quick to hug the bearer of good news. It was the second victory of the afternoon. Rowtina thought how odd it was to feel as good as she did for a couple of total strangers.

Osceola stood and called for announcements. All the women

looked at one another, but nobody made one. "Then, we'll close," Osceola said, and they all reached for each other's hands. Rowtina hated to have to hold Lucy Antiglione's hand after watching her lick her fingers even more during the meeting, but she had no choice. Osceola bowed her head and began, "Let the circle be unbroken," and the other women joined in, "till we meet again." There was a moment of silence before Nelda called out, "Now where's my cake?!" and everyone laughed.

Osceola served homemade red pound cake with butter pecan icing on porcelain dessert plates she'd brought from home. Lucy teased her, but Osceola said, "There wasn't any way I could serve my red pound cake on paper plates and say it was in my Kara's honor. This is a special occasion, darlin'." Rowtina was curious to know what exactly had happened to Kara, but she wasn't sure there'd ever be an appropriate time to ask.

"I've got to go back downstairs," she apologized to the other four women. "Thank you, though." Osceola, Egyptia, and Lucy said good-bye as though there were a silent pact not to ask if she'd come to any future meetings.

When Nelda walked her to the elevator she told Rowtina, "Don't feel like you have to make a decision about being a member right now."

Rowtina wanted to say something like "Oh, I'm sure I'll join," or "I don't see why I wouldn't," but she didn't want to lie.

"I'd like us to be friends, Rowtina. I want you to know you can call me if you need something." Nelda gestured back toward the meeting room. "You can call any of us."

On the ride back down to the emergency room, Rowtina decided it wasn't likely she'd be calling to tell Nelda or anyone else about Turtle. Leaving a husband who beat you like Lucy Antiglione or finding a man who would never think of it like Egyptia—that was one thing. But none of those women in that circle of chairs on the seventh floor would understand what had happened between Turtle and her. And even if she thought one of them might, Rowtina wasn't the type of woman to talk about something like that out loud. Before she'd been old enough to comprehend its full meaning, Sylvia Mention had impressed upon her, "There's only one thing worse than thinking the preposterous. That's wasting your breath and other people's time saying it out loud."

No, Rowtina had no choice but to keep what was or wasn't happening with Turtle to herself. And hope it didn't drive her crazy.

Three

It was exactly one week later that she actually saw him. After nights of waiting, too anxious to sleep, she came home from Mount Olive and barely made it to the bed. She felt as though she'd been drugged. Dropping her coat on a chair, she stepped out of her shoes. As much as Rowtina wanted to perform her nightly ritual of bathing, oiling, and perfuming, she didn't have the strength. Crawling between the covers fully clothed, she thought, *I'll get up in a little while, I just want to lie here for a minute.* She placed her hand on Turtle's pillow. When she awoke suddenly an hour later, it was because she felt his presence close by.

Standing in the bedroom doorway, he had on half the clothes he'd owned. Clothes she'd packed but couldn't bring herself to donate to Goodwill like her mother kept prodding her to. Shirts—blue, striped, plaid—one on top of the other. Sport jackets, at least two pairs of jeans, his charcoal-gray suit. He'd even put his dress shoes on over his high-top sneakers.

A shaft of greenish-yellow light fell around him as he faced the hallway, carrying the one big suitcase they shared.

"Turtle. Where are you going, Turtle?" *Can he hear me? Why does my voice sound so far away?* "Turtle?"

She'd tried to be louder but still could barely hear herself. He wasn't ignoring her. She knew that. He couldn't hear her, that was all.

"You don't have to go anywhere, Turtle. This is your home. Are you mad at me? Did I do something wrong after the accident?"

Rowtina tried to throw back the sheet, to get up so that she could go to him, but she couldn't move. He turned toward her now, looking over his shoulder into the bedroom. She still couldn't see his face, but she could feel his eyes on her. He was saying something to her, something important, even if he wasn't using words. But she couldn't understand what it was.

Turtle turned back toward the hall and began to move. He always moved slow, but determined. It was Rowtina who hurried from one moment to the next as though trying to get through them before they could consume her. Turtle would tell her, "You about to rush through your whole life, Rowtina." The first night they'd made love he'd said, "I'm gonna teach you how slowing things down can make all the difference."

He was moving away from her more slowly than she'd ever seen him, but with a grace she didn't recognize. Turtle wasn't ever what Rowtina would have called graceful. Deliberate, but not graceful. Tonight—or was it morning?—he moved as if he were partnering his own shadow, slow-dancing out of sight.

Leaping from the bed, she ran to the door. He was traveling down the stairs, away from her and the rooms they'd made their home. The light around him was dense as fog. When he reached the bottom of the stairs, Rowtina could make out only the top of Turtle's winter cap. He seemed to be looking up at her.

Do you want me to come with you? I will. Oh God, Turtle. Wait for me. I'll come.

Rowtina hurried down, but as she got to the last step, the door of the brownstone swung open and shut noiselessly. A sliver of light, a coattail of mist, and he was gone. Rowtina stood for a moment in her apartment hallway. "Dammit," she moaned to the closed door. "What is it you want me to do, Turtle? I would've come with you if you'd let me."

Rowtina looked down at her stocking feet. *It's a miracle I didn't break my neck coming down these stairs. Hell, if I hadn't gone to bed with all my clothes on, I'd be standing here naked. Trying to catch up with Turtle.*

She decided she'd describe it to Nelda as a dream, a very realistic dream—to see if maybe Nelda had any ideas as to what it might mean. Rowtina waited a few days, changing her mind three or four times. *But,* she reasoned, *everybody talks about their dreams, don't they?* Rowtina dialed Nelda's floor.

"Six North. Nurses' station."

"Nelda?"

"No. Would you like to speak to Nurse Battey?"

"Yes, please." In a few minutes, she heard Nelda's voice calling out an instruction to someone as she picked up the phone. Rowtina almost changed her mind again and hung up. But the image of Turtle in the light, moving through the doorway, came back to her and she gripped the phone tighter.

"Nelda?"

"Yes?"

"It's Rowtina. I'm sorry to bother you, but I wanted to thank you for inviting me to the meeting. I thought everyone was really very nice."

"Are you going to come back?"

"I've been thinking about it."

"Good. We'll be in the same place, same time this week."

"Oh. Alright, then."

"Rowtina, are you okay?"

"Yes. Why?"

"Because you sound funny."

"No, I'm okay. I am. I've just been having these uh, dreams."

"What kinda dreams?"

"I can't really talk about them now, Nelda. We're really busy down here."

"Did you want to have a drink maybe? When we get off?"

"A drink?"

Nelda laughed. "You can have an ice cream sundae if you want, and I'll have the drink."

"I didn't want you to think there was anything wrong, that's all. 'Cause there isn't. Really. They're just dreams."

"That's fine. You can tell me about your dreams, girl, and I'll tell you about mine. I'll meet you right outside the Twelfth Street entrance."

"Yes," Rowtina answered. "I'll be there."

When Rowtina stepped outside, Nelda was already waiting for her under the HOSPITAL/NO PARKING sign. *She could be a model for those ugly uniforms,* Rowtina thought, observing her. *She looks like she's going out dancing in hers.*

Nelda called out, "So where did you want to go?"

Rowtina looked around. "I don't know. You think there's anything open? It's after eleven."

Nelda cocked her head and frowned. "In the Village? Don't you keep your eyes open on the way to your train uptown?"

Rowtina laughed weakly. "I guess not. I don't know too much about Greenwich Village at all." But she wanted to sound sophisticated just the same. "I'm a Harlem girl."

"Well, shit"—Nelda put her hands on her hips—"I'm a Harlem girl, too, originally. But it never hurts to expand your horizons." The nurse sauntered down the street a little ahead of Rowtina. "Actually, I know a place over on Tenth. It's real relaxed and quiet so we can talk."

Nelda led her around the corner and upstairs into a little café called Just a Bite's.

While waiting for someone to come over and show them to a table, Rowtina caught a glimpse of herself in the mirror, standing next to Nelda. Nelda's thick, straightened bob was jet-black with a shine that probably made people wonder if it was perhaps a wig, or at least dyed. Rowtina could tell for sure it wasn't a wig, but she was fascinated by the color. Under certain light, at the hospital, for instance, it looked almost blue. Even if Rowtina ever thought about dyeing her hair, she wouldn't have had the nerve to pick the color Nelda had.

She wore little makeup and could have passed for years younger than the late thirties Rowtina suspected she was. People looked at Nelda when they passed her. There was something about her and the way she angled her head with those glasses on top like a tortoiseshell crown that made people acknowledge she was moving toward them and then away. Nelda didn't seem to notice. But to Rowtina, who could never understand people bull-dozing into her as though she weren't right there in front of them, walking with a woman like Nelda Battey made it impossible not to compare.

With her own hair brushed back flat against her skull, Rowtina was her mother's "honest-looking" daughter. That, Sylvia Mention had explained to her, meant that what a man saw when he looked at her was exactly what there was. "Two perfectly good eyes, a nose that doesn't call attention to itself, and a mouth that is neither too large nor too puny-lipped. It's all really quite decent."

As far as Rowtina could remember, "decent" was the highest accolade Sylvia Mention had ever bestowed upon her. When Rowtina graduated from Rosa Parks Public High School with honors, Sylvia Mention allowed that Rowtina had gotten "decent" grades. The morning of her wedding, the mother of the bride told her daughter in her ivory-colored silk dress that she'd managed to look "very decent after all." When the ceremony was over, she whispered to her, "I only pray you'll have a decent life with your UPS man." Rowtina was sure that no matter what she aspired to in her life, in Sylvia Mention's eyes she would achieve a level of "decency" at best. With Turtle Washington, Rowtina knew in her heart she'd achieved more than that without trying.

Nelda eased into the booth across from Rowtina. "So tell me what the hell is going on. What are these dreams you're having?"

Rowtina crossed her legs under the table, then uncrossed them again. "Oh, they're not so strange, I guess. They just seem so real." She looked at Nelda, even now trying to decide if she really wanted to tell any part of it to her, even if it wasn't the complete truth.

"Look," Nelda said, "I'm here and I'm curious as hell. I come from a family that believes dreams can turn your whole life around."

Fine. Rowtina decided to take that as a sign. "The first one happened the night of Turtle's funeral. In it, he came back to our bed. He put his leg on mine and I could feel it, I swear."

Nelda held her head with both hands, listening attentively.

"I had the strongest sense that he was trying to tell me something. But he left before I could figure out what it was. For about a month, I hoped I would have the dream again. And that this time I'd be able to understand what it was he wanted."

"Is that why you're upset? Because the dream hasn't come back?"

"I was. But then I had another one." Before Rowtina could continue, a waitress appeared at their booth, startling her. The waitress immediately offered to come back in a few minutes.

"It's not necessary," Rowtina told her. "I'll have a cup of Earl Grey, please. Nelda, are you going to have a drink?"

"I am indeed," Nelda quipped. "Glass of Chablis, please."

"Would you like ice?" the waitress asked her.

Nelda looked at the woman as if she'd asked in a foreign language. "Absolutely not. If it's not cold, just bring me another white wine that is. Your choice.".

The waitress giggled. "White wine, no ice, and an Earl Grey," and she left them alone again.

"Now," Nelda said to Rowtina, "the second dream."

"Yes," Rowtina began. "This time was different. This time Turtle had on layers and layers of clothes, like a homeless man. And he was carrying our suitcase, the only one the two of us own. He stared at me like he wished I was smart enough to know what he was trying to tell me. And then he left."

Nelda told her, "That's how dreams are, honey. The pieces don't always fit. Now, you know who's good at interpreting dreams?" Nelda continued. "Osceola. You should tell her about these. You should come to the meeting this week and talk about them."

Rowtina was becoming frustrated with her plan not to tell Nelda they weren't really dreams at all. "But I *am* talking about them," she snapped. "Right now. With you." She was immediately embarrassed by her tone and tried to soften it. "The thing is, Nelda, I have had dreams my whole life, like everybody has. When I tell you that these feel more real than any other dream I've had, I mean it."

Nelda leaned back into the corner of the booth, studying Rowtina above the dark glasses perched on the bridge of her nose. "Rowtina, are you saying you've been having visitations? That Turtle's been coming back to you? Is that what you're saying?"

Rowtina was startled. It was the last thing she'd expected from Nelda. "Do you believe in visitations, Nelda?" she whispered.

Nelda laughed. "I've never had one, thank God—I'm not sure

I'd know what to do with one—but it doesn't mean I don't think somebody else could have one."

"Do you think it's possible that Turtle is trying to tell me something?"

"If you think it's possible, honey, then so do I."

Rowtina looked at her suspiciously. Was Nelda making fun of her?

"I do!" Nelda affirmed, as if reading her suspicion. "It's not the first time I've heard about spirits returning. My grandmother used to say she had 'em walk right into the room, sit down across from her, and be so real she could see the other person breathing."

"But Nelda, why can't I understand what Turtle's trying to tell me?"

Nelda reached to comfort her. "Maybe he should be patient with you until you can. In the meantime, I'm telling you, you should come to the meeting and talk about it. This is the very thing the Sisterhood is meant for." She raised her unused fork for emphasis. "Dedicated to."

Rowtina folded her napkin in half, then in half again, frustrated. "How could that be, Nelda? It's called Leave Him and Live. I don't know how you think that applies to me, since by the time I met you, it was Turtle who'd already left."

"What I'm telling you is that what I can't answer, those other women might be able to." Nelda twirled a band of onyx and pearls around her finger. "They have a helluva lot more experience listening to men than I do. And how can they help you if you don't ask?"

Rowtina would have welcomed an answer from Nelda, if somewhat cautiously, but the idea of presenting something so intimate to three other strangers was out of the question. "What if I wait until he comes to me again, maybe tonight even? If he does, I can ask him once more what he wants. I'll listen more carefully this time. Then it will be between the two of us. I won't have to tell anyone else, and you can forget I ever brought it up. And if not, I'll think about telling the whole group."

Pushing her glasses up on top of her head, Nelda combed her blunt-cut helmet of bangs from under them. "You're lying, Rowtina Washington. And you shouldn't lie to your Auntie Nelda. Your Auntie Nelda wouldn't lie to you."

Rowtina went home, bathed, and oiled herself. She put on one of the gowns she'd bought after Turtle began his visits to her. Pale lavender with a low neckline, it was edged in satin and held up by two small bows at the shoulder. Rowtina sighed at the reflection of herself in the bathroom mirror. Maybe Turtle had come back and seen her through different eyes. Perhaps this new Turtle didn't feel the same way about her. No, that was wrong. She could tell by his touch that first night. It had been three months now, but she'd have to remember and trust that memory until he came back again.

She turned off the bathroom light and walked slowly into the darkened bedroom. At her side of the bed, Rowtina knelt and folded her hands in prayer. *Let him come tonight. And please let me be smart enough to understand whatever signals he may be sending.* She opened her eyes and smiled, trying to look calm and confident on the chance she was being watched.

Slowly, she stood, untied the first bow, and waited. He had to know how much she wanted to please him. He'd always known before. "Don't you think I know I'm lucky?" he'd asked her once after kissing her, one lip at a time, then both together.

When she untied the second bow, the lavender gown slid past her shoulders to the floor. She stepped out of it, tossed the comforter aside, pulled back the sheets, and slid into bed. Turning away from his side, she curled into her half-moon, then slowly stretched one leg out behind her.

I'd do anything you asked me to, Turtle. You know that, don't you? She'd never been so still. She held her breath until she thought she'd faint.

Two hours later, Rowtina sat up and clicked on the light. She leapt out of bed and pulled her lavender nightgown on, knotting the ribbons tightly at the top. *Alright, Nelda. You win, dammit. I'll ask those women. And hope one of them can tell me anything at all about what the hell is happening to me!*

Four

Three days later, Rowtina told Dina she was taking an early dinner break. She rode the elevator up to the third floor, went through the chapel, stopping for a moment to ask herself, *Are you sure?* She decided the answer was yes and went into the meeting room.

Nelda was putting the folding chairs out. "Hey, girl," she smiled at Rowtina. "I was hoping I'd run into you here."

"It's 'cause you said I was lying to you." Rowtina rolled her eyes dramatically. "Hurt my feelings."

She sat down next to Nelda. A few minutes later, though, when Osceola announced, "Let's get started, shall we, Sisters?" Rowtina prayed to Turtle, *Please don't feel like I'm putting our business out to strangers.*

Osceola continued, "I believe you asked to speak first, is that right, Lucy?"

Rowtina hadn't requested a place on the agenda. She looked to Nelda to say, "I forgot about the rules. I don't have any right to speak today."

But Nelda nodded slowly at her, a sign of encouragement. Lucy sat on the edge of her seat with her bare legs stretched out in front of her. "The little prick is following me," she told the other women. "He's threatnin' to do some serious damage if I don't go back to him."

"What do you mean 'serious damage'?" Egyptia was horrified.

"He said it wouldn't matter how many new teeth I had if my whole face was smashed in."

"Good Jesus, help us!" Egyptia stood in her plaid pantsuit looking like she was either ready to run or take Sal Antiglione on herself. "Forgive me, Lucy, but you married a real bum!"

"Oh, he's as low as they come, alright." Lucy pulled up her skirt several inches, exposing even more of her doughy thighs. "Nasty as a wart on the devil's ass, but he don't scare me one friggin' bit."

Osceola and Egyptia both looked a little taken aback by Lucy's imagery, but all the women seemed stirred by her unbroken spirit.

"What you should do is speak to the police, Lucy," Nelda said. "You've got to get an order of protection."

"You really think so, huh?" Lucy seemed to be looking to Osceola for her response.

"I think you ought to do whatever you can to see that the man doesn't hurt you again," Osceola said quietly.

"Well, I am worried about the dickhead trying to bust up my teeth for the second time!" Lucy let out one of her barking cigarette laughs, but it sounded more frantic to Rowtina than amused.

Nelda pulled a pad and pen from her bag. "I'll take down all the details right now, so you'll already have them when they question you." For the next twenty minutes, she quizzed Lucy and took notes. Lucy repeated Sal Antiglione's threat to her and dozens of other details. Rowtina was impressed with Nelda's thoroughness. Nelda and Lucy made a date to go to the police together. Osceola and Egyptia offered to arrange their schedules to go along, but Nelda said it would be easier to deal with the police if it were only the two of them. There was silence in the room for a few moments, as if they all needed time to digest the seriousness of what was happening. Rowtina wished she had offered to go to the police with Lucy like the others had. But it all seemed too personal, exactly the kind of thing her mother always warned against. "People need their privacy so they can make a mess out of their lives all by themselves. Once you put your nose in it, you got your own mess and theirs on top of it."

Osceola looked at Egyptia, Rowtina, and Nelda expectantly. "We'll move on, then," she said, "with the next order of business." Egyptia raised her hand timidly.

"I feel pretty foolish making this announcement today, after what's been happening with Lucy and all. But Luther and I are having our engagement party in a couple of weeks and I expect each of you to come early and stay late. You're my family and I want you there every step of the way. Right up until the wedding night." Egyptia put her hand over her face and giggled as if she were thirty years younger. Then she took her hand away and said, "I'm serious. You all know I like being married and you didn't try to make me change my mind about it. You just said, 'Get a better fit this time.' So that's what I did."

Lucy shouted, "Wha'd you say, Egyptia girl? You tried him and he fits?"

Nelda laughed, Osceola shook her head like she couldn't believe Lucy had said it, and Egyptia put her hands back over her face. Lucy coughed with laughter till she began to choke.

"We'll all be there, I'm sure." Osceola was still shaking her head in disbelief. "You let us know what you need and we'll figure out who should do what. Now, is there anything else on today's agenda?"

Nelda looked sharply at Rowtina. Rowtina swallowed hard. "I do. I mean, I have something."

"By all means, Rowtina. Please," Osceola said.

Rowtina pushed herself to the edge of the chair, thinking it would make her feel stronger, less nervous, but it didn't. Her legs trembled and even when she put them together they simply continued to shake, except as one unit instead of separately.

"Nelda thought it would be good for me to talk about my husband. Turtle. I think you all know that my husband died, but I don't think any of you know how." Rowtina had surprised herself. She hadn't realized she was going to tell the Sisterhood all of the details. But it suddenly seemed she couldn't talk about Turtle coming back to her without saying how he'd left in the first place. She put her hands on her knees to keep them from shaking. "My Turtle was driving his UPS shift," she began, "when he had a stroke. He drove through a Safeway window and three other people were killed."

She told them everything. The ages of the cashier and the two boys who didn't have enough time to get out of the way of the truck to save themselves. She told about the morgue and the funeral—of being so glad that night that Turtle had come back and how she'd waited for him to return.

She was ashamed, she said, that when he did she couldn't understand what he was trying to tell her. "I told Nelda, and Nelda said I should tell all of you," she concluded, flushed with nervousness. "She thought you might have some idea of what I should do."

No one had laughed at her yet and Nelda even looked proud of her. Somehow, telling the whole story to these women loosened something in Rowtina that startled her. She looked to each of them and believed that what she'd told them was safe.

"Turtle is trying to tell me something, I'm sure of it." She looked out above the women's heads and shrugged. "I'd do anything he wants, but I swear I don't know what it is." She patted perspiration from her forehead. Osceola reached across the circle to give her a handkerchief.

The other women stared at Rowtina expectantly. Osceola broke the silence. "Well, darlin', this is the first time anybody here has had your particular situation. Mostly, what we've been dealing with around here are men who are alive. Flesh and bones alive. Sometimes they seem to appear out of nowhere"—she gestured toward Egyptia—"and sometimes they're hellishly bad, but they're definitely alive." The rest of the women laughed. Rowtina smiled shyly.

Lucy Antiglione volunteered, "What you oughta do is move outta that apartment."

Rowtina put her hand over her own mouth, as though she could stop Lucy's.

"That's right," Lucy nodded confidently, underlining the judgment she'd just made.

Rowtina swallowed and said louder than she'd said anything till that moment, "But I don't want to move. There's no reason for me to." As much sympathy as Rowtina had felt for Lucy only minutes before, she was burning to tell her now, "I didn't marry a man who beat me, Lucy. I'm not trying to avoid my husband."

"Huh! I'd say waitin' around for a husband you already buried is a sign you should try some new surroundings." Rowtina could tell by the other women's faces they thought Lucy had crossed a line. But it was Nelda who spoke.

"Rowtina's heard your opinion, Lucy. She can consider it. If she wants to."

Lucy murmured, "Only saying what I thought made sense." She sat back looking deflated, tucking and retucking her hair behind her ears.

So, Rowtina thought, *I've made a jackass of myself and been insulted by a total stranger.* All she wanted to do was go back downstairs to the emergency room until the end of her shift, then take the train uptown to the privacy of her own apartment. Sisterhood be damned. Nelda was wrong. There was nothing these women could do for her that she couldn't do for herself.

She stood to leave, even though she knew the meeting wasn't officially over for another fifteen minutes. Osceola stood also to face her. "Don't you run away from here mad at us, Rowtina."

"I'm not mad at anybody," she lied, feeling the other women's eyes on her. "But I can't stay today. We're short-staffed downstairs." Rowtina made a beeline for the door.

"Rowtina!"

Nelda was behind her. Rowtina stopped and turned around without moving toward her.

"You threw them a curve, that's all. And even though you didn't like Lucy's suggestion, she offered it trying to help."

Rowtina wanted to walk away before she said something to Nelda she knew she'd regret. But she steadied herself and said evenly, "You're right, Nelda. It was a suggestion. I'm sure Lucy meant it to be a great help."

Rowtina walked toward the elevator. When the doors closed and she was finally being carried down to the main floor and away from the Sisterhood of Leave Him and Live, Rowtina huffed aloud in exasperation, "I tell them all that so somebody who didn't have any better sense than to marry a criminal psychopath can tell me to move out of my apartment, my home. I'll tell you what they're a sisterhood of—they're a sisterhood of crazies. Sittin' around in a room minding each other's business. They're a pack of biddies, busybodies, and crazies!"

An intern whistled as he waited for the elevator. When the doors opened, Rowtina was still talking to herself loudly, angrily.

The intern was inside the elevator pressing the fourth floor button when she blurted, "Can you believe them, Turtle? Can you believe them?"

The intern turned back to her. "Pardon me, ma'am?"

"Oh, I'm sorry," Rowtina told him, feeling ridiculous. "Just going over a little difficulty I've been having."

It was Sylvia Mention who'd first warned her daughter, "Whenever there's a bunch of females claiming they get together for the Good of Womanhood, run for the nearest exit and don't look back lest you turn into a pile of horse shit."

In her junior year in high school, Rowtina submitted her own name for membership in the Marian Anderson Club after not being able to find a member who would sponsor her. On the day the new members were to be announced for the coming semester, Rowtina waited anxiously outside the classroom where the club met twice a month on Thursdays. She stopped Elizabeth Oliver, the club secretary, as she was leaving the meeting. "Did you get my nomination? I put it in the club mailbox. Did you get it?"

Elizabeth kept her gaze fixed straight ahead. "So you were serious? Nominating yourself? We thought somebody was playing a stupid joke."

"Why?" Rowtina asked her. "Aren't you allowed to nominate yourself?"

Elizabeth Oliver kept walking for a moment in silence. Then she said, still without looking in Rowtina's direction, "Look. The Marian Anderson Club has a reputation to uphold. The boys call it 'Fox Central.'"

Rowtina nodded, eager to show Elizabeth that she was aware of all that the Marian Anderson Club represented.

"We're the best-dressed, most attractive girls in Rosa Parks. We all have boyfriends. Some of us have boys out of state driving the thruway all hours of the night just to get to us." With this, she glanced at Rowtina for a mere second.

"I know this sounds snobby," Elizabeth continued, "but we can't afford to let everybody in. It would destroy how special the club is." She tilted her head back, clasping her books higher on her chest. Rowtina stared at how her wrists crossed each other like sculpture and the way she spread her fingers across the back of her notebook like she was drying her nails.

Elizabeth cocked her head to the side as though she could look out at Rowtina through the top of it without having to turn to her directly. "Didn't you say in English class that you were interested in nursing?"

"I am," Rowtina responded, thinking that surely a miracle was about to occur.

"Then you should join the Nursing Club."

"Oh." It wasn't at all what Rowtina had expected to hear.

Elizabeth sighed deeply. "You may think you want to be in our club now, but you'd actually hate it. We don't do anything but gossip about who's getting laid and how big the dick is that's doing it. You'd be bored out of your mind." She turned and smiled right at Rowtina, then floated down the hall. Rowtina understood perfectly how a boy from out of state could drive on the thruway all night to see her. Everything that Elizabeth Oliver had said made absolute sense, at least for an hour or two.

When Rowtina confided to her mother that she'd nominated herself for membership, though, she also felt compelled to lie about the reason she'd been turned down.

"The dean is restricting how many members a club can have, and the Marian Anderson Club is already way over the limit. They said they can't accept any more new members this year. But I'd probably get nominated for sure, if they could."

It was not Sylvia Mention's way of parenting to have heart-to-heart talks with her daughter. But perhaps she saw that something was missing from Rowtina's face, something that had been there when she'd left that morning. It was gone from her cheeks, her mouth, and most particularly from her eyes. Her daughter had been robbed. Beaten and stolen from. If no one else could see it, Sylvia Mention could not miss it. That theft so outraged her, she spoke to Rowtina that evening in a way that probably surprised both of them.

"Marian Anderson Club, huh? Don't have a thing on the Women's Auxiliary of Harlem. And I know because I was a member. The Women's Auxiliary was to 'encourage the betterment of black women in Harlem.' Whatever the deuce that meant."

Rowtina was fascinated by her mother's face, both childlike and ancient, eyes lowered, but clearly not out of shyness. There was a strange, crooked smile that Rowtina couldn't remember having seen before.

"I was a proud, committee-joining, dues-paying idiot for three years. Right up until the Twelfth Anniversary Wine Sip for members and their husbands at Saundra Channel's on 115th Street.

"Tillie Johnson and I were lugging refreshments from Tillie's apartment to Saundra's, so I told your father to go on ahead and meet me there. Getting into the cab, Tillie drops a bowl of potato salad on the curb and insists on going right back upstairs and making a new batch. We don't get to Saundra's for another hour.

"Once we do, I'm still teasing Tillie about martyring herself over some potato salad and I look around Saundra's living room, asking if Win hasn't shown up yet."

Rowtina was especially interested that the story included her father, Winston Mention. Her mother made few references to him. When she did, it was clear from her tone Rowtina was not to try to belabor the moment by pressing for any further details than her mother was willing to provide.

"I'd say ninety-eight percent of the members were in that room with their men, staring at me, asking if anyone had seen my husband." Sylvia Mention's smile seemed to grow even more crooked. "I remember looking at all of their faces and thinking that there must be something wrong with my hair, or maybe my lipstick was all over my front teeth. They looked like they were all pretty amused, but nobody wanted to be the one to say it.

"Then, Cheryline Scott sneers something like, 'Go on back and put your coat down. Win's back there taking care of the coats.'"

Sylvia Mention sat down and then stood right back up again. "All those hussies and their fellas, too, seemed to be looking down at the same gaping hole in the middle of the floor. Half of them were looking mortified and the other half looked like they were trying not to bust a gut. I went back down the hall to Saundra's bedroom.

"The closer I got, I could hear Win was not in there collecting his thoughts. I open the door as slowly and quietly as I can. But he wouldn't have heard me if I'd come in on the A train with brakes screeching.

"Him and Carrie McKee and the Jelly Roll herself, Doris Peoples, are in the middle of Saundra's bed. Carrie and Doris have their dresses up around their fat waists, rolling around on people's winter coats, for pity's sake. Win has his face buried in the middle of Carrie McKee's . . . chest, making this awful snorting sound. And all three of them. Laughing. He does the same thing to Doris. Only this time he's neighing like a damned drunken horse. Then he sits up on her big belly with his licorice legs dangling on either side of her. He's grinning and pulling on her like he's milking an old cow, yelling, 'Titties! Titties! Titties!'

"They all seem to think it's the funniest thing since slapstick. Until Carrie McKee happens to glance into Saundra's mirror and sees me staring back at her."

Tears of rage and remembered humiliation trickled down Sylvia Mention's cheeks. Rowtina felt a sudden sorrow for her mother so sharp that she had to catch her breath and sit down. But as she watched, the look on Sylvia Mention's face changed to something she'd never seen before.

"I reach behind me for the first thing my hand can find. Hoping it'll be large and heavy. As it turns out, it's a crystal bowl Saundra keeps her face powder in. I aim for Win, but I miss him completely. Cut Doris across the forehead. There's blood and face powder flying everywhere. All over the three black pigs and covering the whole Auxiliary's expensive winter coats from top to bottom."

The crooked smile wasn't crooked anymore. Sylvia Mention was beaming now as if she were about to be crowned Queen of New York City. Every member of the Women's Auxiliary of Harlem would have to line up and bow right down to the curb.

"I told Win, 'You better get up, get some clothes on your rusty behind. You got some packing to do.' I told him I'd take my time getting home, which meant he had about an hour. If he wasn't gone by then, I was going to call in some favors to help him out of our apartment. Coward that he was, by the time I got home, he was packed and gone without leaving so much as a note of apology."

Up until now, Rowtina knew only that Winston Mention had left his wife and child. She had not known why or even when exactly. To hear her mother hold the Women's Auxiliary of Harlem at all responsible was at once shocking and yet not surprising at all.

Nevertheless, between the Marian Anderson Club and the Women's Auxiliary, Rowtina decided it was probably better not to trust that she would ever be accepted into membership by any club or organization of women, no matter their age or color. Sylvia Mention and her daughter Rowtina were simply not cut out to be club-joining women. And there was no shame in that.

Five

The next day, Rowtina screened her calls at home before going to work. *I don't want to ruin my day speaking to any of those kooks from that meeting!* When she went into work, she tried to appear too busy to answer the phone, even though she knew how unfair it was to Dina. Eventually, Dina bellowed, "You got a call, Rowtina. Do you wanna take it?!"

"Who is it?" Rowtina scowled.

"I didn't ask," Dina answered her briskly.

Rowtina dawdled getting to the phone. Hopefully it wasn't Nelda. And if it was, maybe things were too frantic on the sixth floor for her to wait. She'd have to hang up and save Rowtina the aggravation of having to talk to her.

"Emergency room. How may I help you?" Rowtina asked in her most formal sounding voice.

"Rowtina!"

Rowtina knew at once it wasn't Nelda. *Please don't let it be who it sounds like.* Cautiously she answered, "Yes, this is Rowtina speaking."

"It's Lucy Antiglione. Hope you don't mind me callin' you at work like this."

Rowtina pinched her lips and glared up at the ceiling. When she looked down again, she realized Dina Tamaris was watching her through the office window from the station they shared.

"It's not that I mind, Lucy. It's that we're really busy right now."

"Yeah, well, I know you're prob'ly still upset about what I said at yesterday's meeting. I only wanted to tell ya when you're through bein' upset, I'm hoping we can still be friends."

Rowtina was hard put for an answer. "Thank you for calling, Lucy. I better get back to work now."

"Rowtina!"

Rowtina brought the receiver back almost up to her ear. It wasn't difficult to hear Loud Lucy. "Yes?"

"Take down my number, in case you ever feel like talkin.' You got a pen?"

Rowtina squinted in exasperation. "Yes. I've got one."

"717-637-4904."

Rowtina scribbled on a Mount Olive admitting form. On the line where it said "Patient's Name," Rowtina wrote "Loud Lucy Antiglione." For "Patient's Telephone Number," Rowtina put the numbers in the appropriate boxes. Then she went back and underlined "Patient" several times.

"I know you think I'm the last person you'd ever call right now, but just in case."

Rowtina managed to murmur, "Thanks, Lucy" before she hung up. She ripped the form with Lucy's telephone number from the rest of the pad, tore it in half, and stuffed the pieces into her pocket.

Rowtina thought she saw Nelda as she was leaving the hospital that night. She couldn't be certain because she was too near-sighted and the woman was coming through an exit several feet away. In the event that it was Nelda, Rowtina stopped suddenly, called out "Oh no!" and pretended to frantically search her bag for something she'd forgotten. Then she turned and ran back inside to the elevator. Rowtina tried to think of what to say if it was Nelda and she caught up with her. The elevator seemed to be coming from the other side of the world. When she finally got up the nerve to take a peek back, the woman who might have been Nelda wasn't there anymore.

It's a good thing too! Rowtina scowled. *If she'd had the nerve to come waltzing up to me, I'd have told her exactly what I've been thinking. Sylvia Mention gave birth to one child. I've been forty years without any meddling sisters and I don't need any now!*

Coming up out of the subway at the corner of 145th Street, she saw the revolving red lights a block away, like enormous fireflies dancing in the blue-black sky.

No, she told herself. Rowtina started to walk faster, then broke into a half-run. *Calm yourself. No need to run. It can't be what it looks like.*

When she turned onto 146th, she saw the trucks in front of number 637. "No!" Her neighbors were out on the sidewalk, in the street, or leaning out of windows, most of them in nightclothes. Rowtina mumbled "Excuse me" a hundred times trying to get through them, further down the block. She heard herself saying, "It's my house. Please excuse me. It's my house." Then she stopped. There wasn't any blaze. There were thick hedges of smoke, too much for her to make out her building or the ones on either side.

She got to the wooden horses lined up several buildings away from her own. When she tried to duck under them, a fireman blocked her. "Lady, lady! Back up!" He put his arms out to stop her, accidentally punching her in the chest, knocking the wind out of her. They stared at each other for a moment, but the fireman only repeated his order for Rowtina to move out of the way.

"That's my house! That's where I live!" she shouted at him. *It's all that's left.*

Someone gripped her arm. She couldn't take her eyes from the wall of smoke, and the floor where her apartment would be if she could see it.

"Mrs. Washington."

She recognized the voice. It was Mrs. Lasley, her landlady. Rowtina didn't want to look directly into Mrs. Lasley's face. The dead calm in her voice was frightening enough.

"What happened, Mrs. Lasley?"

"It's 635, honey."

"What?"

"It's 635. It's not our building," Mrs. Lasley repeated in a low whisper. "I feel damned guilty to be so relieved. But I am."

Rowtina thought for a moment she'd float up into the stifling smoke. She couldn't get enough air and she couldn't keep her balance. Mrs. Lasley, even shorter than Rowtina and at least twenty-five years older, grabbed her so tightly it hurt. She held her until Rowtina's legs straightened again and her eyes were open and focused.

"It's not us?"

"No, honey, it's not us."

Rowtina heard herself sigh. *Oh, Turtle, it's not us.*

It was hours before the two women could go into their apartments. Number 635, next door, was gutted. The front of the brownstone was charred, with windows broken and the door an ominous black hole. Still, it stood, a scorched, abandoned shell the fire had rummaged through, robbing anything of value.

No one was killed, although three of the residents had to be rushed to the hospital for smoke inhalation. When Rowtina saw her neighbors lifted into the ambulances on stretchers, she'd feared like the others around her that they were dead or dying. The word came back and flew quickly up and down the block that all of the old people were alive. One of the ambulance men had said he was sure they'd be alright in time.

Mrs. Lasley offered to have two of the other women from 635 stay with her, for the night at least. Rowtina extended the invitation also, to Miss Betty Jones, who looked to be about a hundred and seven and couldn't stop her tears from falling. "I don't know what's the matter with me," Miss Betty told Rowtina. "I know I'm alive and I'm grateful for it. I don't think I'm crying, but my eyes and my nose keep running and I'm shaking like I got the St. Vitus."

Miss Betty refused Rowtina's invitation to stay the whole night because she was sure her sister would want to come down from the Bronx and get her. She agreed to borrow a dress from Rowtina and wait for her sister in Rowtina's living room, quietly sipping tea and weeping without meaning to.

When Miss Betty and her sister, Esther, left the apartment, Rowtina went to the street with them to help them get a cab. Miss Betty stood across the street from the building she'd lived in for twenty-three years. In a small treble voice she said, "I guess I have to start over. Simple as that."

She got into the cab, her cheeks still moist, carefully lifting the skirt of the dress Rowtina had lent her. As the cab drove down 146th Street, Rowtina continued to stare up at the burned-out house next to the one she lived in.

She went in, bathed, and washed her hair. She pulled out every drawer in her bureau, wondering if she only imagined that her blouses and underwear reeked of smoke. When she opened the drawer that held Turtle's clothing, she put her face into it and inhaled deeply. She sat back on the floor astonished, but pleased. *Only you, Turtle. They still only smell of you.*

Sitting on her side of the bed, Rowtina looked over at his. He had to have known about the fire. She knew he did. *Were you trying to warn me when you came before?* She looked over at the dresser again. *What else were you saying with all those clothes on, and the suitcase?*

Sliding down onto the sheets, she stared at his pillow. *Do you want me to move, Turtle? Is that what you want?* She turned away and stretched her leg out behind her. "Listen, honey. You've got to help me. You've got to make this easier. If you want me to move out of here, then come tonight. Please. Come tonight and make it plain."

This time not even an hour passed. Rowtina was barely asleep. There he was, in the doorway, on his way out. He had on all those layers of clothes again, the clothes she'd just held and been thankful were safe. And once more he was carrying the suitcase.

Rowtina asked as loudly as she ever could when she saw him this way, "But why? Why do you want me to move, Turtle? Why do you want me to leave our home?"

He didn't turn back toward her. He moved slowly through the doorway. The hallway was pitched into darkness when he left. Rowtina lay very still, somehow knowing there was something else coming, some other moment waiting to join this one.

When she heard the voice, she couldn't place it at first. She knew it was supposed to be Turtle's, but it didn't sound like him at all. It was high, tinkly, like the treble keys on a piano. "Simple. Simple as that."

Rowtina thought she heard a car door slam and the car drive off, as close as the foot of her bed. She had a memory of watching a trembling gray dot through a backseat window, disappearing down the street. And she knew then whose voice it was that said, "I guess I have to start over. Simple as that."

She pictured Lucy Antiglione in the meeting the day before. "I think you ought to give yourself a chance to start over."

Rowtina reached for Turtle's pillow and whispered into it, "Alright, Turtle. I understand."

Six

She awoke on her back, cradling his pillow. Slowly, she opened her legs—stretched her big toes toward the opposite corners of the bed like he'd taught her, the first time. She pushed his pillow further down on her stomach, wrapped her thighs around it, imagining it growing heavier. One hundred, two hundred pounds heavier. And darker. Slippery with sweat. Even so, she lifted her own weight against it, holding it tighter. The first time he'd told her, "All we gotta do is work together. I listen to you. You listen to me. And we'll both know all we need to know." So that's what she did. She listened. She heard him. And on a Sunday morning when she should have been up already dressing for church, he carried her out of herself like he always did. And she was grateful.

"Nelda?"

"Yes?" A sleepy voice answered the phone.

"It's Rowtina." She remembered it had only been hours since she'd tried to avoid the woman she thought was Nelda at the hospital.

"Rowtina. Are you alright?" Suddenly Nelda sounded wide awake.

"We had a fire last night."

"A fire?! My God, Rowtina, where are you?"

"I'm in my apartment. I'm fine. The fire was next door."

"You're sure you're okay?"

"Really. I'm alright. It's still a little smoky in here, that's all."

"Shit, Rowtina. You scared the hell out of me."

Rowtina smiled, thinking how unlikely it was that she'd be somebody who could scare the hell out of Nelda Battey.

"I'm sorry, Nelda. I was actually calling to thank you. For trying to help me. I know I didn't act like I was real grateful, but I've been thinking maybe Lucy was right. I'm . . . well, I think I might be moving."

Nelda didn't miss a beat. "Really? Maybe you should come downtown. There's an opening coming up in my building."

Rowtina was startled. "Oh, I couldn't see myself down there in Greenwich Village, Nelda. Not me."

"Why? What are you afraid of?" Nelda snorted loudly. "Baby, you got to stop sending fear out ahead of you, or you won't get out your door."

Rowtina could hear Nelda changing positions with the phone. She imagined her waving her long fingers through the air, scrunching up her full lips like she did when she thought she was making an especially impressive point.

"I didn't say I was afraid, Nelda. What I meant was, I didn't think I'd feel very comfortable in Greenwich Village." She made "Greenwich Village" sound like Alabama during slavery. *How many black people actually live in Greenwich Village, Nelda? Besides you?* "I've lived in Harlem my whole life," Rowtina told her. "I'd have to really think hard about moving someplace so far away."

"That's exactly why you should move down here," Nelda said flatly. "Something brand new. So you'd stop thinking of forty as your whole life."

Rowtina held the phone away from herself and made a face at it. "I'll think about it," she mumbled.

"Wha'd ya say, honey?" Nelda yelled.

Rowtina put the phone back up to her mouth. "I said I'd think about it."

"Good. That's all I'm asking."

"And Nelda?"

"Huh?"

"Don't even think about telling me to bring up moving to Greenwich Village at a meeting. I'll make up my own mind, without the help of the Sisterhood, thank you."

"You'd be making up your own mind anyway, darlin', whether you brought it up at a meeting or not. But I got the message. Message received."

Greenwich Village. Sylvia Mention didn't curse often, but Rowtina knew that's precisely what her mother would do if she ever brought the idea up to her. It wouldn't be as bad as when she announced her engagement to Turtle—nothing could top that—but she'd curse a move down to Greenwich Village, Rowtina was sure of it.

Easing down into her bathwater, Rowtina listened as a radio choir sang. It was the third Sunday of the month. At her mother's church, the church Rowtina had grown up in, the Third Sunday meant baptism. The Third Sunday Women of Jordan would sing a cappella as the minister lowered someone into the baptismal pool,

"I've been loved,
I've felt the power,
I've been loved,
I've felt the grace,
Something's changed me,
Changed me,
Now I'm different,
God's perfect love shines on my face."

Third Sundays meant sitting next to her mother trying to figure out how anybody could feel so good about being different. Rowtina knew what it was to feel different when she suddenly grew taller than the tallest boy in her sixth grade class. They called her "the giraffe," and she threatened to have her father beat all of them up, except they knew she was lying because he'd been gone since kindergarten. Patrice Clark told her, "You wish you had a father to beat even one of us up," and the whole class laughed.

Her mother told her in her first year of high school that "necking, petting, and letting boys feel on your private parts were for girls who were common, ordinary, and you must remember, Rowtina, you're different." Rowtina couldn't think how she was different or if she wanted to be.

It wasn't until she started to think of herself as middle-aged that Turtle Washington told her, "You, you there, Miss Rowtina Mention, you be movin' me like no other woman I've met yet. Sweet Jesus! You a woman set apart, you know that?"

If she'd understood him correctly, this man was saying yes, she was different—and she could be certain from the way he said it, this time different was good. It was her miracle to be different. What Rowtina didn't know how to tell Turtle was that maybe he was the something that had made her so.

In her tub on the third Sunday of the month, Rowtina sang to herself, "Something's changed me—changed me, now I'm different," but she ached so deep, she was sure whatever had been made so wonderfully different eight years ago was escaping out and into her bathwater.

Somewhere between the verses, the phone rang.

Four rings means I'm supposed to answer . . . that's two . . . three.

She reached for her towel.

Four.

Stepping out of the tub, she ran into the bedroom. "Yes?"

"You busy?"

Rowtina was surprised to hear Nelda's voice again.

"No. I'm—" She stopped herself from telling Nelda she'd jumped out of the tub and was standing in her bedroom, naked and wet.

"Listen, why don't you think about coming downtown later this afternoon? You could see my apartment. And maybe I could find the super and get him to show you the one that's available."

"I—I don't know, Nelda. I guess I could. But I told you I don't think I'd ever move down there."

"Doesn't hurt to look, though, does it?"

"I guess not. But I couldn't stay long. Maybe we should make it some other time, Nelda."

"No. I insist. Come and stay as long as you can. Don't eat a big breakfast, though. Cause I'm gonna feed you a fabulous lunch. "

"Please. Don't cook. I'm not . . . I won't be . . . it's all the smoke from the fire last night. It's made me nauseous."

"Well, then don't stay in there. Go out and get some fresh air! Give me about an hour and then come on downtown."

Rowtina strode back into the bathroom, threw the towel across the sink, and plunged back into the tub with the force of a marine scuba diver. With only her head above water, she laughed loudly.

"Turtle?! You think I'm out of my mind to go down there?" She sank even further into the tub, the sudsy water edging up under her chin. "Maybe Nurse Nelda Battey is flirting with me."

Shoot. Rowtina laughed at herself. *Nelda Battey's not even thinking about your old silly behind, Rowtina. She's prob'ly got whoever she wants and a couple more besides. Here you are thinking you're so irresistible, she can't wait to get you inside her four walls.*

By now, only Rowtina's forehead, eyes, nose, and mouth could be seen amid a white blanket of perfumed suds.

I'm out of my mind, huh, Turtle? Out of my mind.

Seven

If Nelda made a pass at her during lunch, Rowtina missed it. True, they each had three glasses of Chablis, two with lunch and another while they waited for the lemon sorbet to thaw for dessert. They were drinking the third glass and sinking into the plush cushions of Nelda's cinnamon colored sofa when Nelda started singing along with Erykah Badhu to "Tell Tyrone." When she went to turn it up, Rowtina began to harmonize with her softly, thinking Nelda wouldn't hear her. Nelda turned from the CD player and smiled. "See how you are. If you hadn't had three glasses of wine, I never would have known you could sing like that."

That caused Rowtina to feel brave enough to ask about the photograph of Nelda and another woman in the center of the mantelpiece. From where Rowtina sat, she could see that in the photo Nelda was wearing her nurse's uniform under a black coat with a dramatic high collar. The other woman, although about the same height as Nelda, was much smaller and fragile looking. She wore a deep burgundy colored coat and a wan smile. Rowtina said as casually as she could manage, "That woman in the photograph standing next to you, she's really pretty."

"She was beautiful," Nelda answered.

"Was?" Rowtina repeated.

"That's Kara," Nelda told her. "Osceola's daughter."

Rowtina suddenly felt a little less comfortable. The room was suddenly darker and the music seemed trite and inappropriate.

Nelda arched her back and lifted her head as if she were facing a sudden wind.

"How long ago was it?" Rowtina asked cautiously.

"That the picture was taken, or that she died?"

Rowtina couldn't bring herself to say "died." Nelda answered her thoughts anyway. "It was taken the same year she passed."

"What . . . was it?"

"Cancer."

"And Osceola decided to start a group in her memory?"

"Eventually. She started Leave Him and Live because she thought Kara's life might have been saved if she'd left the man she was with. She wanted to encourage other women not to make the same mistake." Nelda leaned back into the sofa. "Osceola says sometimes you gotta grab a hold of your sister, or your daughter, whoever is put in your path. You gotta hold on to 'em tight till they can see the road."

Rowtina knew she might be trespassing, but she wanted to know more about Kara McQueen. "Were you . . . very close?"

Erykah Badhu had stopped singing. Nelda looked at Rowtina and spoke into the stillness. "At the time, I think if I could have died instead of her, I would have."

"Why does Osceola think she might have been saved?"

"Who knows if she could have? She was married to a crazy man. Told Kara cancer was a white man's disease they let get outta control. Said he wouldn't spend a quarter paying for white men to pretend to cure her when it wasn't in their hearts to help any black woman stay alive."

Suddenly Rowtina felt more than tipsy. She was vaguely dizzy and short of breath. "But what about you and Osceola? Couldn't the two of you help her?"

"Osceola spent every damned dollar she had. I didn't even

meet Kara until I was assigned to her. And by then, she was seven months away from death."

Rowtina went up to the mantelpiece and stared at the photograph.

"Where was this taken?"

"At the corner outside Mount Olive, the day she went home. Both Osceola and I tried to convince her to stay, but she wouldn't. I asked her if she was tired of fighting. She said, 'No. But I'd just as soon fight at my mom's house. At least she'll feed me so I'll think I'm winning. They feed me Cream of Wheat here. You can't think you're winning when all they feed you is Cream of Wheat.'"

There was a tapping on Nelda's door. A man's voice called, "Nurse? You ready?"

Nelda stood up and tossed back the rest of her wine. She ran her fingers across her lips as her eyes searched the room. Rowtina understood. *She's looking for her. Like I look for Turtle.*

"Nurse? You ready to show your friend the apartment?" The voice outside was louder, more insistent.

Nelda finally opened the door and leaned back toward Rowtina at the same time. "This is my super, Crazy Harry. What do you say we take a look at some real estate, girl?"

A white man no more than five feet tall, with a thick accent that Rowtina didn't recognize as anything but foreign, led them to a garden apartment right below Nelda's. There was a back entrance with a fairly decent-sized patio and a surprising patch of grass. Rowtina stepped out into the May first air and could almost imagine herself on a lawn chair reading *Essence* under a wide straw hat.

"Who else uses this patio?" she asked warily, not that she was even considering renting an apartment in Greenwich Village.

"Only you and whoever you want to be using it with you." The super grinned suggestively. "They're supposed to put it on the market next week. I thought maybe a lady friend of mine was interested, but . . ." He shrugged.

"I'd take it myself if I wasn't too damn lazy to pack up my whole apartment." Nelda still had the shadow of Kara McQueen across her face, but the familiar crispness had returned to her voice.

The super scratched his stomach, then started on his scalp. "It'll be a lot more expensive when they turn it over to a friggin' agent."

"Well? Say something, Rowtina," Nelda prodded. "Do you like it?"

"Of course I like it, Nelda. It's not that I don't like it."

"And the garden?"

"It's wonderful. It is."

"And ya gotta admit it's reasonable for where it is," the super said, flicking dandruff from under his nails, "here in the Village and this little backyard and all."

It was as though the two of them had rehearsed their pitch before Rowtina came downtown. She nodded to them both, several times to each, and smiled so big she felt silly. "Yes, it's very reasonable."

"Then taaaaakkke it!" Nelda roared.

"I can't just take it," Rowtina heard herself whining. "I have to think. I really have to think!"

"Well, come on in and think, then," Nelda deadpanned, then turned and strolled majestically from the patch of grass to the door.

The super grinned. "Think about being out here on a hot July night with that special Mr. Hoohaa. Oooowheee!" He called out to Nelda, "You know where to find me, Nurse Lady."

"Nurse Lady"? Rowtina shook her head disapprovingly. Not to mention "Mr. Hoohaa."

Once they were back upstairs in Nelda's apartment, Rowtina

thought she should thank Nelda politely and leave. But she didn't want to. She couldn't remember the last time she'd sat in someone else's home, slipped off her shoes, and eaten a meal prepared especially for her. She'd felt good for a few hours with someone who liked to see her laugh and told her so. Knowing Kara's story made Rowtina feel closer to Nelda and to Osceola. She wanted to tell Nelda, "It's alright to wait for her. I wait. There's no shame in waiting."

Because there was more she might have said and couldn't, she announced simply, "I've got to go home now."

"Well"—Nelda eased to the edge of her armchair—"I'm glad I could convince you to come down from Harlem and see me, at least." She stood, pushing her bangs back off her face. Without the frame of hair or covered by any makeup, Rowtina was startled to see that Nelda was lovely, actually. "Lovely," Rowtina remembered, was a word her mother was fond of, but Sylvia Mention was very sparing in her use of it. She had, as she liked to say, "standards that were higher than most people's." But Rowtina thought her mother would agree this time. Nelda's face was softer than Rowtina had ever seen it. Her eyelids were smooth and naturally bronze-colored, not their usual shadowed, smoky gray with hints of silver. Her full lips a rich, pinkish brown instead of the near-black let's-get-down-to-business plum she painted them. Rowtina felt that she was seeing Nelda for the first time, really, that afternoon. And Nelda was lovely.

As Rowtina started down the block toward the subway, Nelda called out, "Why don't you ask Turtle what he thinks?!"

Rowtina could barely believe she'd heard it. She turned to face Nelda.

Nelda shrugged. "No harm in asking, is there?"

It was a combination of things, but isn't it always? It was knowing that Turtle was laughing at her—she could hear him laughing—at how wrong she'd been about Nelda lying in wait for her. It was thinking of him making it plain, the night of the fire, that she should move, start over. But hadn't Nelda said that even Kara McQueen went someplace familiar when she wanted to feel like she was winning? *Why do I have to leave Harlem?* Not that it made her feel like she was winning, exactly. *I haven't felt like that since . . .*

But maybe that was exactly the point. You need to go someplace else, Turtle was telling her. You could feel good again if you picked up and started over.

By the time she was standing on the uptown platform, waiting for the A train, Rowtina knew for sure. She fumbled through her bag, hurried to the middle of the platform where she found a working pay phone. Punched in the number and placed a quarter in the change slot for her three minutes. When the phone picked up on the other end, she could hear Erykah Badhu again in the background.

"Nelda?"

"Wha'd you forget?"

"I decided I'm going to try."

An A train was coming into the station on the downtown side. Rowtina put her hand over one ear.

"Try what?"

"Try living someplace besides Harlem. Can you hear me?"

"I can hear you. And that means?"

"That means could you please tell your super I'm interested in the apartment."

"Are you serious?" Nelda seemed to be shouting now.

"I think so. Yes. I'm serious."

"Because I was thinking about it after you left, and if you're worried about me being so close, I want you to know I like my privacy too. I won't be down there bothering you."

"Nelda, I'm not worried!" Now Rowtina's train was pulling into the station. "I've got to go. I'll see you tomorrow."

The train doors would have closed, leaving Rowtina on the platform, had it not been for two teenage girls who each stuck a thigh in the way, forcing the doors to reconsider. Rowtina jumped on and thanked the girls.

Slightly embarrassed at the attention she'd attracted, she hurried to the other end of the car. Sitting in one of the two-seaters at the tail end, she perched on the edge, trying to make sure the woman who was already there still had enough room. The woman glared at her. Any other time, Rowtina would have jumped back up and stood all the way to 145th Street rather than listen to the woman mumbling under her breath about "no damn room for two." But this evening, Rowtina decided she was going to enjoy her ride. And if the woman needed some additional space, Rowtina thought, *She can stretch right out there on the floor, for all I care.* She laughed to herself. *We've got to concentrate on moving, don't we, Turtle?*

The woman fidgeted, half sighed, half grumbled something unintelligible.

I'm not thinkin' about you, lady. Rowtina rolled her eyes and chuckled again. *I'm thinkin' about making a move.*

Eight

"I'll be glad to pay you half of next month's rent since I'm leaving on such short notice," Rowtina offered Mrs. Lasley.

"Sugar Plum, Mrs. Lasley can take care of herself. Didn't Mr. Washington show you the lease he signed for the two of you? You already paid me a month's security when you moved in. We're square as far as I'm concerned."

The only other notice Rowtina had left to give was to her mother. She waited until the day before she was supposed to move to call. Sylvia Mention's first response was to ask Rowtina if she'd lost her job. When Rowtina replied no and followed up with where it was she was moving to, her mother asked if she'd lost her mind.

"Whatever would possess you? Are you having some kind of breakdown?"

"No, Mama, it's just something I want to do."

"Well, there are dozens of things I want to do, but being of sound mind and reasonable intelligence, I consider the repercussions."

"What repercussions, Mama? What could happen from me moving downtown?"

"You're a black woman, Rowtina. Why would you even want to move to Greenwich Village? There's nothing down there for you. No friends, no food—where would you get your hair done?"

Rowtina looked into the mirror and ran her hand over her hair. It was short and soft. She'd actually thought about not having it straightened, wearing it natural to see how she liked it. Maybe if her mother wasn't around to demand somebody "straighten up that nappy hair . . ."

"I'll think of something, Mama. I'll take care of my hair."

"I'm beginning to wonder if you're in a state of mind to take care of yourself. Maybe you should have come here with me after your husband died. I knew you were pretty shook up, but now I'm thinking it's worse than I thought."

For one ugly moment, Rowtina imagined herself in her mother's tiny apartment on 168th Street being told what to wear to work, to rethink her nail polish and dull her lipstick color.

"Mama, I'll be fine. I will."

"Well, I don't think you will be fine. You won't tell me, because you'll want to save face. But I want you to know you can come back and stay with me if you need to. People make mistakes. I've been here for you when you've made mistakes before. I'll be here for you again."

"Yes, Mama. Thank you."

Rowtina hung up and thought, *That's it. The rest will be easy.* She studied her hair in the mirror again. *How do you think it would look natural, Turtle? You think you'd like it?*

The following Sunday, Egyptia and her fiancé, Luther Wooldridge, picked Rowtina up from 146th Street. They followed the Harlem Deluxe Movers truck downtown to Ninth Street where Nelda, Osceola, and Lucy were waiting. There, everyone except Nelda and Rowtina drank iced tea in Nelda's apartment until the three moving men had placed Rowtina's belongings in the new apartment. Nelda and Rowtina stayed downstairs supervising. After the movers left, the members of the Sisterhood offered to help

Rowtina put things away, but she refused to let them. She appreciated their help and told them so, but the truth was, the taped cardboard boxes contained the world she'd shared with Turtle. That world was still too private for her to allow people who didn't even know Turtle to handle and possibly even damage.

When all of the boxes had been neatly stacked and the furniture placed in various positions in each of the small rooms, Nelda called the rest of the Sisterhood down to present Rowtina with a gift for her new home.

Rowtina, already surprised at their generosity in wanting to help her move, unwrapped the large, hard square, shyly aware that the women were watching for her reaction. When she'd untied the bow and stripped away all of the wrapping paper, she struggled for words to say anything at all.

The gift was a framed print of a mahogany colored woman standing naked in a tub, bathing herself. Next to her was seated a much older woman who was clothed.

"It's called "Susannah in Harlem," Nelda announced, "by Romare Bearden." She chuckled. "I was kinda thinkin' maybe it could remind you of old times."

"It was Nelda's choice," Egyptia said. "It's not what I would have chosen for you. I kept trying to tell the others I didn't think it was your taste, but no one would listen."

"We hope you like it, though," Osceola ventured nervously.

"The truth is," Nelda drawled, "yes, I am entirely responsible for the choice. I went ahead and picked it out. If you don't like it, I'll give you the receipt and you can get something you like better. Maybe you and Egyptia can go together." She shot a raised eyebrow toward Egyptia, who suddenly took her fiancé's arm and seemed to shrink into the side of him.

"But I do like it," Rowtina told them. "I just don't know where I'll put it yet. You'll all have to come back once it's up and tell me what you think."

"You don't want that. Trust me." Lucy walked over to "Susannah in Harlem" and studied it more closely. "You put it where you want and enjoy it. To hell with what we think."

"Amen! Now can we please go out and celebrate?" Nelda put her arm through Rowtina's and gestured toward the door.

Rowtina suggested Just a Bite's. It was the only thing vaguely familiar in the neighborhood, other than Mount Olive.

"We can do that today, but eventually I've got to expand your horizons," Nelda laughed.

Strolling the streets of Greenwich Village, Rowtina already missed the churches, beauty shops, bars, and rib joints that had surrounded her for so much of her life. The music, smells, and voices were so different than what she'd come to take for granted as her home. Most of the faces on Ninth Street were white. Rowtina wondered if she'd ever really feel comfortable in this neighborhood. For the first time, she realized how much Harlem was really New York City to her. Downtown may as well have been a suburb, the suburb where she worked, but after work she'd gone back to the city she knew best and loved, the city of Harlem.

From a huge billboard on Twelfth Street, two adolescents stared out over the neighborhood. They appeared to be a boy and a girl. Both of them had waist-length blonde hair that fell over their chests, though, so neither of them appeared to have even a suggestion of breasts. Their ears, noses, and lips were studded and ringed. Rowtina couldn't tell what the models were advertising. Underneath their images was an Italian word she assumed was a fashion designer's name or perhaps a store she'd never heard of. Under the Italian word, it said, "LIVE THE LIFE YOU DREAM OF."

Rowtina stared for a moment at the two enormous blonde teenagers pouting down at her in their ringed and studded nakedness. *Turtle, I hope I didn't get my signals crossed. I hope I didn't misunderstand what you were saying.*

On the corner of Tenth Street, as the women headed toward Just a Bite's, Lucy stopped dramatically and turned her ample frame toward the window of a hair salon. The shop was empty except for a stylist trimming his customer's hair with the grace of a matador in the ring.

"Sheeeiiitt! Wouldja look at those buns!" Lucy shrieked.

Everyone looked, including Luther. Rowtina couldn't help but see what Lucy was so excited about. The man's behind was a good deal slimmer than Turtle's, but his jeans didn't hide the fact that it was round, appeared to be firm, and sat atop a pair of long, muscular legs.

"What I wouldn't do for a plate o' ham like that!" Lucy continued to bellow.

Osceola took her by the arm and said, "I'm not about to stand here in the street gaping at that man's behind, Lucy!"

Egyptia and Luther had already moved on. Nelda whispered to Rowtina as they followed Lucy and Osceola, "I see you're back to window shopping. That's a good sign, I guess."

"Don't be ridiculous." Rowtina shook her head dramatically. "I'm not Lucy. I was looking at the shop, not the man."

"Uh-huh," Nelda teased. "I saw ya . . . lookin' at the shop."

Rowtina felt ashamed. She wasn't used to being teased and she was embarrassed that Nelda was right. She had been staring at the man's behind. She'd compared it to Turtle's, and before she could stop herself, she'd pictured them both side by side, naked.

Forgive me, God, Rowtina prayed silently. She fastened the top button of her blouse and tucked it into her pants. *Forgive me, Turtle.*

That night she smiled at how she'd had the moving men place her bed and dresser in the exact same arrangement as the old apartment uptown. *If Turtle followed me down here, it would all pretty much look the same.* "You know I'm down here in Greenwich Village, don't you?" she called out. Of course he did. Would he come? Turtle used to tease her about working down in the Village. "I bet you get all kinda weirdos comin' into that emergency room, don't ya? Those kids with the porcupine hairdos, and all the men with boyfriends, women with green hair and fifty million rings all over their faces. Why don't you get a job up here in Harlem taking care of your own?"

And Rowtina told him, "You get to drive all over the city in your truck, Turtle—you ask to be put on a different route every chance you get 'cause you don't want to be looking at the same thing every day. Well, I get on a train and go down to Greenwich Village. Those people need emergency care the same as our people need emergency care. I guess if I thought people needed me more up here than down there, I would work up here. But the Village is where they hired me. Riding from Harlem to down there makes me feel like I'm doing some traveling every day. And I like to travel."

What she didn't tell him was how the good part was traveling back home again, to him.

I didn't think I'd ever move down here, though, Turtle. It certainly is starting over. You gonna come tell me you think I did the right thing? The least you could do is come give me a sign I did the right thing.

Nine

Egyptia Nelson, at fifty-three, was giving herself an engagement party with all the giddy excitement of an eighteen year old. For the next two weeks, the only business she brought to the Leave Him and Live meetings were her lists of what an appropriate gift might be, should any of the Sisterhood decide to give her one. No one ever talked about this being her third wedding, least of all Egyptia. What she repeated continually, though, was Luther's version of being love-struck at the sight of her. "Luther says the very first time he passed by my classroom, he looked in and couldn't believe his eyes. He says he knew if somebody hadn't already snatched me up, he had to marry me." Egyptia always ended her story with, "Do you believe that?" The fourth time Rowtina heard it, she happened to be sitting between Osceola and Nelda. Nelda answered just loud enough for them both to hear, "No, but if you believe it, that's all that matters, Egyptia darling." Rowtina began to shake with laughter. Osceola reached around Rowtina to poke Nelda as if she were an unruly child in church. But she could barely conceal her own smile.

When Rowtina stopped upstairs at Nelda's to ask her if she wanted to ride uptown to the party together, Nelda surprised her.

"Of course, we can all go together. I'm bringing a friend, do you mind?"

At least ten questions metered in Rowtina's head instantly, but she stopped herself from asking any of them. Instead she answered, "You know I don't mind. Why would I mind?"

"My friend's never late," Nelda assured her. "We'll come down and pick you up around eight."

"Good. This'll be fun, don't you think?" Rowtina knew she sounded a little too chirpy, but she was determined to let Nelda know that whoever she was bringing to the party was fine with her.

Nelda rolled her eyes. "Considering Egyptia's mooning around like a nineteen year old virgin, it'll probably be like a night in the Twilight Zone."

By seven forty-five, Rowtina was totally preoccupied with trying to imagine who Nelda's "friend" was and why she'd never heard of her before. She assumed this "friend" was a woman. She'd never actually seen anybody Nelda dated before, but she was almost certain Nelda wouldn't be coming to her door with a man. And if it was a woman, Rowtina wanted to be sure she didn't embarrass herself by saying or doing anything ridiculous.

At seven minutes after eight, Nelda called. "We're ready, are you?"

Rowtina answered like the only freshman on the cheerleading squad, yelling "Ready, ready ready!" into the phone.

Minutes later, the knock came. Rowtina tiptoed to the door and listened, but she couldn't hear any clues. This was one of the times she wished she had a peephole she could actually see something through. With an enormous fixed grin for whoever might be standing there, she opened her door.

"Hey," Nelda bounced at Rowtina casually. Next to her was a petite, open-faced young black woman. At a glance, Rowtina calculated that although she looked sixteen, she was probably in her early twenties.

"This is Eleanor Blackshear." Nelda glanced toward her friend, smiling.

"Hiiiiii, Eleanor!" Rowtina extended her hand, but not before Eleanor had thrust hers forward. Rowtina admired her mud brown linen pants and jacket, a contrast to the natural luster of her skin. With her pearl earrings and the single strand disappearing into her white oxford shirt, Eleanor Blackshear reminded Rowtina of a fashion spread she'd seen called "Mixing Business With Pleasure." Rowtina even glanced down to see if she was carrying a briefcase.

"Look at you!" Nelda exclaimed to Rowtina. "Baby!"

Rowtina stopped focusing on Nelda's date and shyly received the attention focused on her. She was wearing turquoise silk. It was the brightest color she'd worn in months, a color she knew came perilously close to being what Sylvia Mention would consider "loud." Nelda encouraged Rowtina to buy the dress after she'd admired it in The Designer's Outlet window. "You're forever pointing out things you want. Standing outside pointing. Why don't you go in and buy it, for heaven's sake. Then you don't have to spend so much time outside the window looking in."

Rowtina knew she liked the dress, but she wasn't sure she wouldn't look silly in it until now. She was used to Turtle telling her what looked good on her, and to hear him tell it, everything she put on did. Tonight was the first time someone else was making her feel she could look more than "decent." If she didn't go anywhere now but to the A&P and back, she'd be quite content.

Nelda was her usual glamorous self in black satiny capri pants and pumps, and a fitted black blouse from which her full bosoms seemed ready to emerge at any second.

On the subway ride uptown, Rowtina tried to ascertain how intimate a relationship Nelda and Eleanor Blackshear were having. There were no clues yet from their behavior toward each other. What she did find out, though, was that Eleanor was a medical student doing research at Mount Olive and that's how she and Nelda met.

"You look so young," Rowtina ventured.

"That's what everybody says," Eleanor sighed playfully.

"She's twenty-six," Nelda said dryly, "but she has a very old soul." Eleanor laughed and took Nelda's arm. Rowtina glanced around quickly to see if anyone was looking. Several people across from them were. Rowtina smiled but stared at her shoes, hoping Eleanor would remove her arm from Nelda's. Almost a half hour later, when the train stopped at 110th Street and they all got off, Eleanor was still cozily holding on. Sooner or later, Rowtina thought, someone would call out something to the three of them and there'd be an awful, ugly fight. She followed the couple out of the subway station, looking behind her and wishing she could feel as jolly as they seemed to. When they were a few blocks away from Egyptia's, Nelda turned suddenly and said, "You know, Rowtina, you were right. This is fun, and we haven't even got to the party, yet. I'm with two stunning women and even if the party's dull as dirt, I'll be in great company!"

Rowtina managed to get out, "Thanks, Nelda. I told you we'd have fun."

The minute the three of them entered Egyptia's apartment, Rowtina began to feel even less comfortable than she had on the subway. She'd never considered that there would be people at Egyptia's party she didn't know. Unlike herself, Egyptia and Luther both seemed to have a whole telephone book of friends and family they'd called or sent invitations to. Rowtina had worn her turquoise dress to look nice for the Sisterhood, as though they would be Egyptia's only guests. What was the matter with her? Turtle always said, "Other people get out and socialize. That's what you oughta do, Rowtina, instead of always waiting here for me to get home."

Looking around Egyptia's apartment, Rowtina wasn't sure

how long she could stay in this room full of strangers. Where were Osceola and Lucy? Where was Egyptia, for that matter? What would she have to say to any of these people if Nelda and her date kept to themselves all night? *I'll give Egyptia my gift and stay long enough not to be rude. Then I'll go home.*

"Hiya, ladies!" From the kitchen doorway, over the music and chatter came the familiar, boisterous tone. Lucy stood across the room in a purple iridescent blouse and a matching skirt that was so short it looked to Rowtina like the ones she'd seen nineteen year old ice skaters wear on television. And, lo and behold, Lucy was wearing stockings, sheer with a lavender tint. She stood for a moment in Egyptia's kitchen doorway, posing. Then she strutted over to them and struck another silly model stance. "Thought I'd give my black sisters a run for your money in the style depart- ment this evenin'," she said huskily. All four of the women gig- gled. Lucy suddenly realized that Nelda and Eleanor were together. "Nelda, who's this?"

"This is my friend Eleanor," Nelda said, putting her arm around Eleanor's waist.

Lucy beamed at Eleanor. Rowtina prayed she'd censor her- self. *Whatever you're thinking, Lucy, don't say it.*

Lucy turned and yelled toward the kitchen, "Hey, Osceola! Looka here. Nelda's got a knockout date and Rowtina's lookin' like Miss African America!"

Rowtina tried to shrink a few inches into her shoes. But Osce- ola was already there, reaching for her with both hands and nod- ding in agreement. "You look lovely, my dear."

Rowtina watched as Nelda introduced Eleanor to Osceola. She wanted to see if she could surmise what Osceola thought about Nelda and her date. But Osceola's smile never changed. If anything, Rowtina thought she could hear in Osceola's greeting, "I hope you're good enough for my Nelda. And if you are, I hope you'll be around for a long time."

"Wouldja look at this place? It's a damn dollhouse!" Lucy gestured toward a cranberry velvet couch in the center of the room. There was an armchair to match, a coffee table with a mirrored inlay, and a room divider that reminded Rowtina of a play she'd read in high school, *The Glass Menagerie.* Every shelf was filled with tiny whales, bears, and birds of glass, all of them vaguely expensive looking, yet none of them attractive or special enough for Rowtina to even slightly covet.

"It would be my damn luck to break something in here and have Egyptia try to put my ass in jail," Lucy quipped, and all of her purple iridescence shook with laughter.

Egyptia swept up to them in a pink lace dress that Rowtina thought sweet, but a little too lacy and a little too pink. It looked like one of the pastel, crocheted dresses on the little black dolls Sylvia Mention collected and put in the middle of her bed.

"Look at all of you!" Egyptia sang out. She stepped back from the other women appraisingly. Her smile tightened when she said to Nelda, "You didn't tell me you were bringing a guest."

Nelda answered quietly, "I hope you don't mind."

"Of course I don't mind," Egyptia told her, and Rowtina suspected she was lying. Egyptia looked at Eleanor with her arms folded, her palms clutching her elbows.

"Egyptia Nelson, this is Eleanor Blackshear," Nelda said very slowly. "Eleanor, Egyptia is the bride-to-be."

"Congratulations. When is the wedding?" The tiny Eleanor lifted her face toward Egyptia's. Waves of what Sylvia Mention would have identified as "half-good" hair fell back past Eleanor's shoulders.

"We haven't decided exactly." A shadow passed over Egyptia's face for an instant before it broke into a startling, electric smile. She said so that the whole room could hear her, "Luther keeps worrying me to hurry up and set a date, so I guess I better hurry up and set a date!"

She moved away from the Sisterhood as quickly as she'd come.

"Shoot," Lucy said in what she probably meant to be a whisper. "Old Luther didn't know what he was walkin' into when he hired on to teach at Egyptia's school. She's gone off the deep end. She thinks she's got herself Sidney Poitier in *To Sir with Love.* Now you take a look over there at old Luther. I mean, he seems like a decent enough guy, but Sidney Poitier thirty years ago when he was all muscley and juicy? Darlins, only if you got a blindfold and earplugs."

Everyone giggled but Rowtina. She thought, *How dare Lucy talk about a man like Sidney Poitier that way?*

"The thing is," Lucy continued, "she's so desperate to get to the altar, if that man don't marry her soon, she'll have to move outta state to save face."

In the small, overdecorated apartment, Egyptia's guests loaded their plates, filled their glasses, and tried to find a comfortable perch for the rest of the evening. Osceola and Lucy went back into the kitchen to help Egyptia serve. Rowtina offered, but Egyptia, who'd become quite sullen and clipped, told her, "The kitchen is crowded enough as it is, thank you. What you might want to do is take Lucy with you to the living room so she won't eat up everything before it gets out to the rest of the guests."

Lucy only laughed, went out and positioned herself at the serving table, where she continued to fill her plate and chat with anyone who stopped by to fill theirs as well. "Try this," she'd advise with her mouth full, or, "I'd pass on that, if I were you. It'll go down fine right now, but in a few hours, no one'll be able to light a match near you."

Rowtina was too embarrassed to stay next to Lucy. She found a place a few feet away from Nelda and Eleanor, who continued to stand very close to each other, seemingly oblivious to the rest of the party.

Luther acted not only as bartender but D.J. The more Egyptia's guests gulped down her special party punch, the more they called out full-throated song requests to him. A few of them danced. Even Osceola and Lucy glided around each other to Al Green for almost half a song. Rowtina watched, pretending to sip a glass of punch that was long gone. Throughout, Nelda and Eleanor continued their quiet conversation with each other, no matter the music or an announcement of a new dish coming out of the kitchen.

"I got one for y'all!" Luther called from the CD player. The sweet molasses harmonies of Harold Melvin and the Blue Notes' "If You Don't Know Me by Now" poured into the room.

Of the Sisterhood, it was probably Rowtina who noticed first. Egyptia and Osceola were in the kitchen, Lucy was chatting at the serving table. Arms around each other, Eleanor's head against Nelda's breast, the couple began to dance, though they hardly moved at all. Eleanor's eyes were closed, her body leaning into Nelda's in a graceful surrender.

Rowtina looked around the room. Now all eyes seemed to be directed toward the corner where the couple was dancing. As if drawn by a huge magnet, Egyptia came slowly out of the kitchen. She glared toward the corner, her whole body rigid. Stalking toward the dancing couple, she passed Luther on the way. "Turn that damn thing down," she shot at him, then she proceeded to Nelda and Eleanor. She stood directly in front of them, giving Nelda little choice but to stop navigating Eleanor around on their private dance floor. Nelda returned Egyptia's glare. Eleanor opened her eyes like she'd been awakened abruptly from a pleasant dream. Harold Melvin and the Blue Notes could still be heard, but Egyptia cut through the melody like a butcher's cleaver.

"I'm sorry, Nelda. I keep a Christian house. And it's not that kind of party."

Someone gasped. Lucy blurted, "Egyptia!" from where she stood at the serving table. Osceola, who'd finally fixed herself a plate of fried chicken and macaroni salad, put it down on the table next to her. Rowtina inhaled deeply, trying to gather strength to do whatever might be needed in the next few minutes.

Nelda, with her arm still around Eleanor, smiled slowly at Egyptia, as though Egyptia had simply announced her apologies that there was not enough macaroni salad to go around. "That's alright, Egyptia. I understand. Thank you for your hospitality."

They were gone before anyone else could move. Rowtina looked over at Osceola. Osceola sighed deeply and walked toward the bedroom. Lucy was still at the serving table with her hands on her hips. "What the hell?" she said, looking genuinely confused. "What the hell?!"

Rowtina put down her glass. She followed Osceola to Egyptia's bedroom, where they'd both left their bags. Neither of them spoke. On the way out of the room they met Lucy, who asked them, "Aren't you two gonna wait for me?"

Osceola answered, "We'll be outside," and she and Rowtina moved toward the door.

When they got there, Egyptia stepped in front of them. "That wasn't necessary. She didn't have to come here to my party and behave like that."

Osceola looked at Egyptia and shrugged slowly. "She was dancing, Egyptia. It's a party. She was dancing."

By now, the music Nelda and Eleanor had been dancing to had stopped. "If You Don't Know Me by Now" was over. As Rowtina, Lucy, and Osceola left, Egyptia's living room was silent, as if the only guests remaining at the long awaited engagement party were Egyptia's collection of glass animals.

Ten

Turtle, it's been a month since I last saw you. In case you don't already know it, I've got tomorrow off. Tonight I can stay up as late as I want and do whatever I want. Anything. You listening to me, Turtle? Anything we want to do, we can do. I miss you. I hope you come.

The next morning—Saturday—Rowtina awoke tired and frustrated. For the first time since the accident, she admitted to herself how irritated she was with Turtle. *I wouldn't be lying here expecting you if you hadn't started this in the first place. If I've made some kind of mistake, please have the decency to tell me so.*

Downtown, there were fewer black men to remind her of Turtle. Coming around the corner, staring at her with his bottom lip between his teeth like he was seeing her for the first time. No uniform in the world could hide the muscles in those thighs and calves. Not wool, cotton, or corduroy. Uptown in Harlem, she'd met a man she'd married, whose calves she'd once massaged with her tongue. And for the daughter of Sylvia Mention that was saying quite a lot.

Last night, coming from the hospital, Rowtina was actually convinced she'd seen Turtle ease up beside her in his UPS truck outside the apartment, like he used to do uptown. She waited to hear his low whistle and flirty baritone. "Old Turtle's got a deliv-

ery, baby. A Rowtina Special. Can't nobody handle it but you."
Instead, a freckled, red-haired woman looked down out of the
truck to check her distance from the curb.

*That's it, Mr. Washington. I'm getting up out of this bed and
going out into the world. Maybe you'd like me to go back uptown
and that's why you're staying away, but before I do, I'm going to
try to enjoy myself right where I am. Somehow.*

Rowtina headed up Tenth Street, thinking she might go to
Just a Bite's and see if they served brunch. Until she'd moved to
the Village, she'd thought brunches were for people on soap
operas, church women and head nurses. In her new neighborhood, every restaurant had a sign announcing brunch.

She was trying to approximate her own version of Nelda's confident stride—part runway model, part championship boxer. The
salon where she and the other women had seen the hairdresser
with the tight butt and the cowboy boots was on this block. She
recognized the two oversized flowerpots with white birch trees in
them framing the doorway.

About a foot from the window, she stopped. She was trying to
decipher the name of the shop written in blue neon script, when
the door opened suddenly in front of her.

"Whatever the question is, I've got the answer."

Rowtina was so startled, she turned her ankle backing away,
stumbling awkwardly. The hairdresser reached out and caught
her by the elbow. His other arm swung around her waist.

"Easy." It was a soft, accented voice.

Rowtina pulled away. "I'm fine." She sounded harsh and she
hadn't meant to. "Thank you."

"Were you looking for someone?"

"No. I just happened to glance in."

"I saw you. I was looking at your hair in the light."

For a second, Rowtina thought he might reach out to touch it.
"My hair?" was all she could think to say.

"Well," he paused, as though he was being extra cautious in choosing his words, "I was thinking how it would complement your face, if you didn't, well, if you wore it exactly like it was meant to be. Like God made it." He laughed. "Except maybe trimmed a little."

Rowtina thought she should keep walking, but she couldn't get her legs to agree.

"I wonder if you would ever have the courage to let a total stranger take your hair into his hands."

She didn't believe he'd said it. It was the kind of line a man might say to some other woman in that accent maybe, but not her.

"I have a hairdresser, thank you. In Harlem." She felt like her mother saying it. She was indignant that this man whom she didn't know had the nerve to criticize her hair. On the street.

"Excuse me. I've offended you."

You're damn right, you've offended me. "I'm not offended. But I do have a hairdresser. Who I'm very pleased with." The truth was, she hadn't gone to the hairdresser's in weeks. She was oiling and hot-combing and rolling her hair herself. Osceola had stopped by the emergency room desk two nights ago to offer a referral out of concern.

"Perhaps you think I have no right to speak of your hair as if it is my business. But"—he shrugged—"it is my business. If you understand what I mean. Hair is my business." He leaned closer, his eyes staring into hers. "And I am very good at what I do." All of this, without for a moment hiding the most even set of white teeth Rowtina thought she'd seen. *Those aren't his. They couldn't be. Nobody has teeth like that in real life.*

He was a very light brown with a halo of big, nappy onyx curls and black on black eyes. As she backed away, Rowtina looked from his starched white dress shirt down his long blue-jeaned legs. She saw how his thighs pushed against the faded denim. She realized she'd never talked to a man wearing cranberry cowboy boots before.

"I'm sure you are very good, and if I decide to do something different—"

"If you decide to do something very different, you should get in touch with me immediately. I am Picasso Alegria." He held one hand out to her. With the other, he pointed above his head to the sign, "PICASSO'S SALON DE BELLEZA."

"And what name should I remember for when you call to make your appointment?"

Rowtina thought for an instant of making something up, but she wasn't a quick thinker. She whispered nervously, "Rootina."

"Rootina," the hairdresser repeated. "That's unusual. Where does it come from?"

"Roowwtina." She enunciated a little louder, feeling ridiculous. "Washington. Do you own this shop?"

"Yes I do. Is it convenient for you?"

"Yes," she answered, before she had a chance to think about not answering. "I live in the neighborhood."

"Then you should consider what I said." He showcased those teeth again and Rowtina backed away.

Go and hold your breath till I let you get your hands on my hair, Mister White Teeth Big Thighs. You got a lotta nerve. Rowtina turned and suddenly felt a soreness in the ankle she'd twisted. *Damn fool man. Almost made me break my ankle.* She tried to strut away from Picasso Alegria without limping, but she thought she must look ridiculous and she wished she'd started wearing her hair natural like she'd planned to. Still, he had a lotta nerve. *Mister White Teeth Big Thighs. Big Butt.*

Rowtina limped to the Shopwell for her dinner groceries. Back in her apartment, she told herself she shouldn't put any weight on her sore ankle, but she still rearranged the corner of her new living room three times. Finally, when it was dusk, she began to cook for herself. It shocked her to think she might be missing the hospital cafeteria. Certainly it wasn't the food. True, Sal and Don behind the counter told her which dishes were sure bets and which she should leave alone. Bernice was at the cashier's table instructing her not to worry about breaking a dollar to give her the exact change. "I'm not worried about a damn quarter," she'd scold her. "If I'm that short at the end of the night, I'll come down to the emergency room and get the damn quarter from you."

In the Mount Olive cafeteria, even if she sat alone, there was always someone at a neighboring table trying to wave her over. Or insisting that if she were going to eat in the cafeteria at all, which was constantly filled with employees, why would she want to eat alone?

Rowtina remembered the nights before the accident when she would call Turtle to remind him there was food in the oven and dessert from the new Muslim bakery on top of the refrigerator. He'd wait for her anyway, and laugh. "I never was one for eating or sleeping alone. Not since I knew the difference." Those were the nights she was especially glad he'd found her.

She washed the single dish and fork she'd used, cleared the place mat from the table, and put it in the cupboard on top of the other one that matched it. In the living room, she tried out yet another arrangement of the table and lamp in the corner.

Then she ran a bath for herself. Lying back under the water with her eyes closed, she sometimes pretended the water might carry her anywhere she wanted to go. Tonight, Rowtina played back her conversation with the hairdresser, imitating his accent. "I wonder if you would ever have the courage to let a total stranger take your hair into his hands."

Standing in the tub, she reached over and pulled the medicine cabinet mirror toward her. Her mother had always kept Rowtina's hair short when she was growing up. "It's not thick and it certainly doesn't grow fast," she told her. "Keep it close and clean. When you have enough money to pay somebody else to take care of it, you can do as you please."

Turtle had always liked her hair short. He'd never said anything about wearing it natural. But then, she hadn't really thought about making such a drastic change until after . . . when she was leaving their home.

Still, clearly the hairdresser was trying to con a potential customer. With those teeth. And those tight pants. It probably worked on other women.

Turtle, you better come on. You see I got a Puerto Rican hairdresser trying to get me into his shop. Rowtina laughed, mimicking Picasso again. *Trying to take my hair into his hands.*

Singing. There is no one else on the street except her. But she can hear a man singing. She knows she's getting closer because the singing gets louder, but no matter how close she gets, she can't seem to understand what language the man is singing in. Now, though, she can see him. It's the hairdresser. It's Spanish she's been hearing, he's singing in Spanish. There is his mouth, his lips several shades of pink to brown, mustache curling over the top.

She looks down his neck to his chest. Gleaming with sweat, his nipples are erect. Sweat drips from the tips of them in slow motion, one drop followed by another. She follows one of the drops as it runs from his chest down his stomach to a patch of black, curly hair down to . . . *My God. He's—*

Rowtina makes herself focus on the ground even though she wants to continue looking past the patch of curly stomach hair. It's only a dream, why shouldn't she look? But she stares at his feet instead. He's tapping his feet in time to his own singing. Wearing his cranberry cowboy boots. Only. She wants to laugh.

The hairdresser is singing in Spanish, in the middle of Tenth Street, naked except for a pair of cranberry cowboy boots.

She sneaks a quick look back up to his mouth. Stares at the mustache again. So thick, she imagines if she got any closer she might lose herself in it like a toddler in a rain forest.

Rowtina turns away and crosses the street quickly. She's afraid she's been seen by someone else waiting on the other side. But when she gets there, no one is waiting after all. *I'm late and he's gone.* She looks down the street. *Did he see me with the hairdresser and leave?*

She'll have to find him and explain she didn't know the hairdresser would be there. There's no way she could have known. She turns to steal one last look, back, across the street. The hairdresser is still there. She has to hurry. *I have to find Turtle and explain.* "Forgive me, Turtle. I don't know why I'm dreaming about this Spanish man. Naked and singing and smiling at me. Forgive me."

Eleven

For a week, Rowtina avoided looking down the block Picasso's shop was on. On the way to the hospital, she'd focus in the opposite direction until she passed the street. Coming home, she'd look straight ahead, refusing to allow her gaze to veer toward Picasso's salon.

She did stop at a bookstore, though, to look up "Salon de Belleza" in a Spanish dictionary. It said two words: "beauty shop." Just like Pearline's Beauty Salon on 136th Street and Rose Edwards's Beauty Salon on 142nd and St. Nicholas. The hairdresser probably thought he was showing her words she'd never seen before and would never know the meaning of. But Rowtina had always been one to find the answer, if she could. It hadn't been hard at all to translate his silly sign from Spanish to English. Even if she didn't speak Spanish, it certainly didn't mean she wasn't educated. She'd taken French in high school. Her mother had insisted on it. They said French was harder. And she'd gotten nothing but A's in it. If the hairdresser's sign had been in French, she'd have translated it to him right then and there. Cocky son of a gun.

It was the Tuesday night of the second week since he'd insulted her and her hair. By the time she punched out from her shift and made it out to the street, it was already quarter after eleven. It certainly never occurred to her that he'd be in the shop at that hour, or she wouldn't have gone back.

She didn't notice the light coming from the shop window. Or was it that she did notice and couldn't remember later on?

The neon sign above the shop cast a theatrical mix of blue and pink onto the white potted birches. This time Rowtina decided there was something actually elegant about the sign, like one you might see above a shop on Fifth Avenue. As she approached the window, she saw the lights inside suddenly go out. Rowtina froze. No, she hadn't realized they were on before now. She started to turn back the way she'd come, but the door opened. A woman with an enormous sculptured mane of red hair and the figure of a fifties movie star stepped out. Then came the hairdresser. Rowtina wasn't exactly in front of the shop—she hadn't quite reached it yet. But he looked right in her direction, as though there was no doubt in his mind that she'd be there, outside his door.

"Finally got up the courage to make an appointment?" Rowtina was dumbstruck. Still in the doorway, the hairdresser told her, "Well, for you, I'll see what I can do." He looked like he was about to go back inside.

"No. I don't want you to do my hair!" Rowtina blurted. The hairdresser stopped, looking back at her. "I mean, I didn't want you to do it tonight—it's too late. I came to make sure I had the name right. Then I was going to call you."

Rowtina was suddenly very conscious of his redheaded companion staring at her, looking perplexed but definitely not as amused as the hairdresser. Picasso laughed as he stepped a little closer to both women.

"I had no intention of doing it tonight. You're right. It's much too late. I was only going to get my book. To see when we could arrange it." He stepped back to the other woman, put his arm around her shoulder. "I'm sorry. This is Mercedes Moreno. She is my partner. Mercedes, this is Miss Rowtina Washington."

Rowtina had already assumed the redhead was his girlfriend. Or his wife. She also felt a twinge that she hadn't corrected him when he'd called her "Miss."

"Hello." Mercedes made the word sound as if it had four syllables. It had nothing to do with an accent. Or perhaps it did, but also with the woman's using "hello" to say more, something in a language Rowtina truly didn't comprehend. Mercedes smiled like a pageant contestant greeting a live and television audience simultaneously, but her tone was filled with something completely different.

"I don't have to go inside at all," Picasso said. "Even without my book, I know I can see you on Saturday. If that's good for you." Rowtina could feel Mercedes studying both of them. It was as if the hairdresser was performing a scene from the same Technicolor movie of the same era she'd stepped out of. His own blue-black hair, too-white-to-be-real teeth, the jeans with the wide, silver buckled belt. The two of them might easily have been costarring with Ava Gardner or Lana Turner, one of those women Sylvia Mention not so secretly longed to be. Her mother, Rowtina knew, would have been instantly smitten by this man, as she was by Cesar Romero and even Desi Arnaz. "There's something about those Latin men," she'd tell Rowtina, and laugh this strange, throaty laugh. "Something south of the border!" Then she'd double over, enjoying her own joke as Rowtina stared at her blankly.

"How could you see anyone else on Saturday? You're booked from dawn until eight o'clock at night." Mercedes's voice was high and sharp, as though she was singing some moody Spanish opera.

Picasso looked at her evenly and said quietly, "I think I know my schedule, Mercedes." He stepped closer to Rowtina. "You can take me at my word. What time is best for you?"

"What I'm saying is maybe you should look at your book after all, Pico. Saturday is crazy for you. Impossible. Every week you say the same thing, 'How the hell did I let this happen?' And every Saturday I say, 'You did it to yourself.' This"—she ges-

tured toward Rowtina—"is a perfect example." Mercedes lowered her voice for the first time as she spoke to Rowtina, as if
explaining how the sun comes out to a four year old child. "He
probably thinks because you have so little hair, he can go
quickly. But, of course, he's a perfectionist. So, for him it would
be the same as if he was doing someone with as much hair as"—
she paused and shrugged—"mine, for example."

Rowtina began to back away. "I can call—"

"I can see you on Saturday. Anytime after three."

Rowtina wasn't at all sure she wanted any part of this. She'd
never had a man do her hair, much less a man who wasn't black.
And she certainly didn't want any trouble from this Mercedes
person, who was starting to remind Rowtina of that gladiator
woman on the television series Nelda watched religiously.

But Rowtina also felt something take her by the shoulders
and turn her directly toward Picasso Cesar Romero Desi Alegria
to say, "I can be here at three-thirty." Adding, "But I don't want
you to cut it. I don't want it any shorter." To which Picasso
answered, "Neither do I."

Mercedes tossed her own elbow length hair again, whipping
the air. She shrugged and laughed. "Well, who am I to tell the
great Picasso how to run his business?"

"It was good to meet you," Rowtina murmured in her direction, and turned away.

"I'll look forward to seeing you again, Rowtina." Picasso's
voice almost swung her back around again. "On Saturday."

He was not a movie star, if she wasn't looking at him. He was
simply a man she'd made an appointment with. Like the dentist.
Or the doctor. That was it. A professional appointment with Picasso Alegria, the hairdresser. Sylvia Mention would be shocked
that a man who looked like him had given Rowtina a second look.
But then, it wasn't likely Sylvia Mention would ever know anything about Picasso Alegria. What would there ever be to tell?

Twelve

At the next meeting of the Sisterhood, Egyptia was very noticeably absent when Osceola decided to begin. "It's possible Egyptia is running a little late, so we'll go ahead and fill her in when she gets here." She closed the door to the meeting room as Lucy said, "There ain't a chance in hell she's gonna show up. She'd have to be crazy."

Lucy had brought a friend to the meeting with her, a black woman half her size who was also wearing a gold and brown Buttered Bun uniform. Lucy introduced the woman by saying, "She's pretty new down at the Bun. The day she started, though, I saw the same bruises in the same damn places I used to have 'em. And that's what I told her. I said, 'I recognize you, Aggie. From the markings.'"

Agnes Williams didn't say much. She sipped on a cup of coffee she'd brought with her and allowed herself to be hugged by Osceola, as Rowtina had at her first meeting. When Osceola asked if there was any new business, Lucy turned to Aggie, prompting, "Hon, if ya wanna talk about anything, this is the time to do it. We may not have answers for ya right away, but we're some smart ass women, so it won't be long." She grinned at Rowtina, and Rowtina realized she wasn't the new member anymore.

"No, no I don't have anything . . . ," Agnes said softly. "I've never been to anything like this before. Y'all got . . . husbands? I mean you got husbands who got bad nerves like mine does?"

"No. We're all different," Nelda answered, adjusting a huge new pair of sunglasses perched on her head. "I can't say that I've had the pleasure of a husband, with bad nerves or otherwise."

Lucy cackled. Agnes looked at her, surprised.

"I'm not laughin' at you, honey, I swear," Lucy told her, squeezing Agnes's hand in both of hers.

At that moment, the chapel door opened behind them. They all looked to the back of the room. There was Egyptia sailing in as if she'd practiced her proud, sure gait and needed a long aisle to execute it efficiently. She was wearing a canary yellow and black striped dress and jacket to match. The stiff collar of the jacket was turned up, giving it a kind of military look. Egyptia's hair was a tight cap of freshly straightened auburn curls.

"Well, whaddya know?" Lucy said. "Egyptia, girl, summer's gotta be comin' soon. You look like a big bumblebee with hair."

Ignoring her, Egyptia strode forward to the circle of chairs. She stopped directly in front of Nelda's. "I'm sorry to interrupt. But I want to say I've been a horse's ass, Nelda, and I know it."

Nelda breathed deeply, looking up at her. "And what do you want me to say, Egyptia? That it's alright, everything's fine?"

"No. You say whatever you want to," Egyptia told her. She stared at the floor like an awkward, embarrassed ten year old, her head wobbling strangely. Then she moved into the middle of the circle and told the others, "After all of you left, Luther told me his brother was coming to the party. With his boyfriend. He and the boyfriend have been together for fourteen years. I've met the brother, but Luther never told me he was . . . like that and I certainly couldn't tell. Luther said if I had any thoughts about not making the two of them feel welcome, he and I were in serious trouble."

"And that's why you decided you were a horse's ass?" Nelda

sneered slightly. "Because Luther put the fear of God into you about giving his brother the same treatment you gave me?"

Lucy sucked her teeth. Clenching and unclenching her hands at her sides, Osceola sighed.

Egyptia put her bag up in front of her like a small leather shield. "I'm older than you are, Nelda. I was brought up in the church. It's hard for me to turn my back on what I know to be God's laws."

Nelda leaned back in her chair as though she was having trouble seeing Egyptia and thought some distance might help. "And what is God's law on two women dancing together at a party? They must've missed that in my Sunday school, Egyptia."

Lucy let out a hoot like a small ship. Osceola glared at her. "We are trying to heal things here, Lucy. Not make them worse."

Egyptia pulled her shoulders up, which made her look swollen, in her canary yellow and black. "Look, I came to offer an apology to you and your uh, the girl you brought to my home. Not because I believe you're right, but because I thought we were all trying to care about each other, overlook each other's weaknesses and faults. How can I stay with everybody feeling so hostile toward me?"

Lucy shot out, "I ain't feelin' hostile toward ya, Egyptia. Right this minute, I'm feeling sorry for ya."

Osceola put her hand on Lucy's arm. "I asked you not to make this any worse. Please respect that." To Egyptia she said, "You're a part of us, Egyptia. There's no walking out. We can fix this. Can't we, Nelda?"

Nelda responded flatly, directly to Egyptia. "I'm not thinking there's anything to be fixed. Nothing broken. Nothing to be fixed."

Egyptia backed away. She sat in the empty chair that Osceola had saved for her next to Rowtina. Nelda continued to stare at her.

The women sat in silence. Rowtina looked into the chapel next door. Since she'd first started attending meetings, she'd never seen anyone in there, except when the Sisterhood passed through. Who used it, exactly, and when? Didn't any of the doctors ever want to go in and pray he'd be able to save somebody's life with a heart transplant or at least keep them alive a little longer? Didn't any of the nurses ever suggest to family members to sit in there and ask God to please stay behind in their son's or daughter's or grandmother's room when regular visiting hours were over? Rowtina could see Egyptia gazing into the chapel now with her mouth turned downward and her fingers clutching at her necklace as if it were choking her.

Osceola cleared her throat, breaking the silence. "Is there any more new business? What about you, Lucy? What's going on with Sal?"

Lucy pulled forward in her chair and, as usual, stretched her meaty, bare legs out in front of her as if it helped her to answer.

"Let's put it this way. He's definitely around. Ya live in a place where rats feel comfortable to come and go as they please, it's pretty shittin' hard to get rid of them. But I'll be okay."

Osceola was persistent. "But is he still threatening you? What happened to the order of protection?"

"Sal ain't afraid of the law." Lucy crossed her ankles. "He told me himself, he wasn't scared of no piece of paper. Didn't matter what the hell it said."

"Well, that is not acceptable," Osceola huffed. "Nelda, what do you think Lucy should do now?"

Nelda shook her head. "You definitely have to report all of this, Lucy. If he comes near you, you have to report it."

"He already came into the coffee shop this morning," Aggie chimed in excitedly. "He's there pretty much every day. Actin' ugly."

"Is that true?" Nelda asked. "Why haven't you said anything? Why didn't you call me?"

Lucy sank further into the chair, her legs jutting into the center of the circle. "Because he's just being Sal. He's only gonna show up more now that I got that damn order. To prove to me it don't mean shit."

At that moment, Egyptia very quietly stood and walked to the door of the chapel. Osceola stood also and called to her. "Egyptia?"

Egyptia turned, looked at Osceola and then at the other women. She looked longest at Nelda. "I have to go," she said quietly. "I have things to take care of. For my wedding." Then she disappeared inside the chapel.

Nelda focused down into her lap for a moment and then up again at Rowtina. Rowtina looked away. *Nelda was wrong. Something has been broken.* She looked from Osceola to Lucy and back again to Nelda. No one had tried to stop Egyptia when she finally went through the chapel door, they simply let her go.

Rowtina thought back to the engagement party and Egyptia in her pink lace, pink nail polish, pink lipstick. Like a little black doll with plastic limbs held together by elastic bands. Rowtina said good-bye to Egyptia. In case that's what it turned out to be.

Thirteen

Well, Turtle, I guess you know I'm going to this Picasso man to get my hair done. I don't want you coming around trying to make me feel like I'm doing something wrong, if you haven't been here after all this time. You've got tonight to either speak up or show up and let me know if you've got a problem with it. Unless you come by tonight and tell me otherwise, I'm going to keep my appointment. Alright? We got a deal?

Saturday morning, Rowtina wished she knew how to not look like she'd spent the night waiting for her dead husband. She stared at her reflection in the bedroom mirror and saw the woman she'd come to recognize—the woman who looked so much older after the funeral and the drive to the cemetery. If she'd waited to see Turtle's coffin lowered into the ground, she'd probably look older still. She believed if Turtle ever came to her with any regularity, she would begin to look like herself again. That wouldn't be the most important thing about him coming back, but she'd definitely thought about it.

She called Nelda. "I'm going to tell you something and you can't tell anyone else. Not even Osceola."

Nelda laughed. "You have my word as a gentleman. I won't tell anyone—even Osceola."

Rowtina rolled her eyes. "May I please continue?"

"By all means."

"I'm going to have my hair done. By him."

"Him?"

"The hairdresser on Tenth Street Lucy made such a fool of herself over."

There was a small silence.

"Oh! You mean the one with the butt. And why would I find it funny that he was doing your hair? Doesn't he usually do black women's hair?"

Rowtina bit her lip. "Well, I don't know if he's done any others', but he wants to do mine. We bumped into each other in the street. He asked me if I had a hairdresser and I said I didn't."

"Right on the spot, huh?" Nelda sounded skeptical, but Rowtina had determined this was the way she wanted to break the news about Picasso.

"That's right. And before I knew it, I had an appointment. It's today."

"Well, that's obviously some head of hair you got."

Rowtina was certain Nelda wasn't buying her story. "I thought about canceling, but I figured why not go and see what he could do. You don't think I'm being ridiculous, do you?"

Nelda was suddenly very matter of fact. "You wanna get your hair done, go on and get it done. You feel like flirting back, you do that too."

"I wasn't flirting, Nelda. I really wasn't."

"That's unfortunate. 'Cause I'd think it was pretty damn good if you were."

"But it hasn't been a year since Turtle . . ."

"The way you've carried on? With all the dreams or the visits or whatever you're calling them. I say, if getting your hair done by Mister Buns takes your mind off what Turtle's doing or not doing, for even an hour or two, I'm all for it."

Rowtina hung up and combed her hair five different ways before she thought it looked good enough for the hairdresser to put immediately under water, which, of course, he would. But when she walked in, she wanted it to look as good as he'd thought it looked the first time. When she'd "bumped into" him and he'd made her feel foolish and angry. And pretty.

At 3:31, she was barely inside the salon when a young Asian woman skittered up to her looking like she'd bounced out of the pages of *Mademoiselle*'s "Everything a Twenty-Something Should Wear This Spring."

"Welcome to Picasso's Salon de Belleza. I'm Christine. Do you have an appointment?"

In the mirrored wall's reflection, Rowtina saw Mercedes staring at her from across the room. Rowtina managed to nod a silent greeting. Mercedes turned back to her client and began cutting so fast, Rowtina thought for sure she could hear her scissors louder than Patti LaBelle wailing through the salon's sound system.

Well, I'm here, Miss Mercedes. I didn't expect you to run over with a dish of mints and a cup of coffee, but I'll be damned if I'm gonna turn around and go back home.

"Yes, I do have an appointment," she assured Christine. "With Picasso. Could you tell him please that Rowtina Washington is here?"

Christine motioned to an area next to her counter where a low, gray leather couch sat before a glass table covered in magazines. "I'll let him know," she purred, and sashayed away like a candy cane in heels.

Rowtina could hear Mercedes's accent and shrill laughter across the room. She concentrated on the pale, shadowy trees with tiny gold metallic birds in their branches hand-painted on the salon's walls. *I don't want him making a fool out of me, just to*

*make her jealous. I don't want to be anybody's Saturday afternoon
amusement.*

She glanced to the side in time to see a UPS truck driving
toward the salon window.

"Sweet Jesus!" she called out. Mercedes and the other women
looked toward the window. Then they stared curiously back at
Rowtina. The UPS driver had pulled his truck to a stop in the middle of Tenth Street, blocking traffic. As car horns started immediately to protest, Rowtina tried to assume a look that said, "That's
exactly what I was screaming about. How could the idiot block
traffic like that on a Saturday afternoon?" Too embarrassed to keep
up the pretense for more than a few seconds, she focused into her
lap and eventually closed her eyes. She ran her fingers over her
wedding band. *What is it, Turtle? I know that's you out there.*

She'd decided she'd leave, without any announcement. She
would simply walk out of a situation she didn't trust and save
herself whatever trouble was surely in store for her if she stayed.

"Oh!" Rowtina jumped, feeling a hand suddenly on her
shoulder.

"I'm sorry to frighten you." She turned to Picasso and the first
thing she saw was his mouth, his mustache, and she remembered
her dream. "I'm glad you came. I want to get you started, while I
finish up with what I'm doing." Picasso leaned over, put his hand
on her shoulder, and sniffed her hair. "You've washed it already.
I'm not surprised. But we're going to do it again. And don't
worry, it won't hurt it."

Picasso led the way toward the back of the salon. He had on a
pair of royal blue silk slacks that seemed to accentuate the
roundness of his behind. Rowtina looked away.

"Mercedes," she whispered.

"Yes." Picasso turned and smiled brilliantly. "What about
Mercedes?"

"Is she your wife?"

Picasso frowned. "Absolutely not. I told you. She's my part-ner. Did you think I was lying to you?"

"No," Rowtina answered, startled at his change in tone. "Just not saying everything."

"I always . . ." Picasso stopped in the area where several shampoo chairs were, "say everything." He reached into a drawer and pulled out a silky fuchsia colored robe, letting it unfold like a master magician. He held it up for Rowtina to step into.

"This isn't something I do anymore, you know. I don't wash anyone's hair, not even my own—I have it done for me. But for you, I'm going to make an exception. Yes?"

Rowtina mumbled, "Thank you," and fell back awkwardly into the chair. She wasn't surprised at all—she expected Picasso would try to seduce her. Only she wasn't sure what that would feel or sound like, exactly. At first, with her head tilted back in the chair, she tried to watch him. She waited, rehearsing what her response would be when he said something too suggestive—or when he slid his hand under her robe, thinking no one saw. She prepared herself to leap out of the chair, throw the smock to the floor, make a moderately loud but nevertheless effective scene, and stalk out of the salon.

He leaned over her and smiled. She clenched her jaw and tried to appear as if she was breathing normally. Turning the water on with one hand, he cupped her head with the other as the warm spray began to soak her hair. The hairdresser's fingers never seemed to release their hold on her scalp. Front to back, they prodded and stroked. She tried to keep her eyes open, but she couldn't. When she looked up at him, he stared back at her with his bottom lip between his teeth, and his mustache glis-tened with moisture. *No. I've got to keep my eyes closed, concen-trate so the tingling in my stomach will stop from moving any further down.*

But when she closed her eyes, it was worse. She could hear

him moaning softly, "Hmm, hmnm?" as though he was asking her something, and she didn't know precisely what it was, but the tingling was definitely moving further down.

"This is something I use that you won't get anywhere else in the city," he told her.

She didn't understand what he was referring to. Maybe she'd misunderstood him. "Pardon me?"

"It's from Paris. It doesn't matter the kind of hair, it makes miracles." He held a tube of shampoo above her so that she could see it. "But you won't know from just one time," he said. "I'd have to do it regularly. And then you'd begin to see how special it is."

"Yes," Rowtina said giddily. "It feels very nice."

She felt him lean in closer. "We're almost there." She held her breath the way she had as a little girl on rides at amusement parks as they were about to come to a stop. When he turned the water off, he held her head for a moment, then wrapped it in a towel and told her, "You can come up now."

She was dizzy when she sat up and even dizzier as he took her hand and helped her out of the chair. He guided her a few steps over to the dryer. She sat as Picasso lowered the dryer over her head and bent down to ask her, "Are you alright?"

Rowtina nodded weakly and tried to smile back.

"I'll be back to get you in a little while," he told her, his face only inches from her own. When he stood and turned to go, Rowtina again looked away rather than watch his behind moving under the blue silk slacks.

She could see Mercedes out in the front room, laughing and waving her comb like a conductor's baton. She looked to be having the time of her life and Rowtina didn't believe any of it. "She's my partner," Picasso had said. *Why didn't she act like a partner? She's probably not thrilled that he "made an exception" and washed my hair—if you can call that washing hair.*

Rowtina concentrated on how long her new pants made her

legs look. She'd decided to buy the black jeans at the last minute, hoping to resemble other women she'd seen in the Village—the ones who looked as though they weren't impressed by anything enough to get dressed up for it.

When she'd almost run out of things to think about other than Picasso, he was there again, lifting the dryer. He combed through her hair with his fingers, tugging at it gently. "Please," he said, gesturing for her to follow him. They went into the main room of the salon, where he led Rowtina to a chair in a corner. She could feel the stares of the other women around her. She knew better than to look in Mercedes's direction.

"Now you are in my chair," Picasso told her, and she felt like she was being introduced to a foreign country by its prime minister. He moved toward her slowly. "I have to show you that what I said is the truth."

"What's that?" Rowtina asked.

"That I am very good at what I do." With his scissors tracing her hairline, he held her earlobe down, his thumb traveling slowly along her jaw, finding its way to her bottom lip. "Don't worry. I'm only going to cut off the damaged." Rowtina thought it was very oddly put, but she understood.

"I see you're wearing a ring and yet somehow I thought you weren't married. Was I mistaken?"

When she opened her mouth to speak, his thumb pressed into the corner of her mouth.

"I'm not. Married." As soon as she said it, she felt ashamed.

For the entire time that Picasso combed, stroked, and cut, he didn't say anything else. That is, he didn't use words Rowtina recognized. But with her eyes closed, his hands spoke to her in another language. It troubled and thrilled her at the same time. And it worried her that she might be more thrilled than troubled.

Then he said, "Rowtina. Take a look at what I've done to you. Tell me if you like it."

She smiled and peered up into the mirror. What Sylvia Mention had often called "a handful of hair," Picasso had so meticulously sculpted that Rowtina was fascinated by how different she looked. Her features seemed more prominent and yet she thought her face looked softer, more elegant. Even though she was wearing very little makeup, she thought surely she seemed . . . well, certainly a close cousin to "attractive."

For a few seconds, Rowtina shuddered at the idea of having to apologize to her mother for what she'd allowed Picasso to do. She glanced down to the floor at her shorn, processed hair. *There's my apology. And it won't get any further than that.*

"You're right," she told him. "You're very good." She looked from her own reflection to his. Beyond him, she could see Mercedes watching.

"And you see I am no liar about something else," he said, with his fingers still on her neck, pressing, massaging. "It complements your face, as I said it would. And when a face is beautiful, it only makes sense to keep beautiful things around it. You agree?"

Rowtina squirmed toward the front of the chair, tugging at her smock. Picasso held her by her shoulders from behind. He untied the smock and pulled it off her easily.

"You're shy. That's very charming. Tell me, shy Rowtina Washington, will I be able to see you outside of my salon?"

Rowtina had trouble getting out of his chair. She couldn't coordinate her feet to hit the floor at the same time she straightened her body. She sank for a moment and reached for her purse.

He continued. "Dinner, dancing, a Broadway play, an opera? Whatever you say."

She tried to sound offhand, clever. "I say, 'It's a very nice haircut. Thank you. Where do I pay?'"

Picasso stood back, letting the smock fall to the side. That matador thing again. In those blue silk slacks and the boots. *Well, I'm getting out of the damn ring.*

"'Very good.' 'Very nice.' I haven't heard this before about my work. So I must apologize because I wanted to give you so much more."

"I—" Rowtina began.

Picasso put his finger to his lips. "Never mind. You said what you felt. You were honest. Weren't you?" And Rowtina knew that they both knew she had not been. "Will you at least think about seeing me and let me call you in a few days?"

Her hands reached for her hair nervously, but she couldn't touch it. It was as if he still had his hands in it.

"I can't."

He studied her. There were more moments of silence between them before he said very quietly, "I'm very sorry if I offended you. That was not my intention. I hope you'll come back some-time."

"I will," she stammered. "I will."

There may have been several pairs of eyes on Rowtina as she stood at the reception desk fumbling with her cash, but there were two pairs she could be sure of. When she went back to hand Picasso a ten dollar bill, he looked at her as if she were heading up a ramp to an ocean liner that would take her away for years. As she walked toward the door, Mercedes called out, "Bye-*biiii!*" like a mocking mynah bird. Rowtina pretended she hadn't heard.

She was practically running down Tenth Street panicked, ashamed. She knew she should have declared to Picasso firmly, "I am married. I am already taken, spoken for, not available. I have a husband." And if she'd said exactly that—"I have a hus-band"—where would she have told him this husband was? *It doesn't matter. I should have told him. Next time I will.*

Fourteen

"You know I had to come see what the hairdresser done to your hair, Miss Rowtina." Nelda had stopped by the emergency room on her way out.

"I like what he did," Rowtina murmured.

"I know you do, baby girl," Nelda teased back. "'Cause what he did looks pretty damn wonderful."

Rowtina wanted to describe to her what had happened in the salon—what Picasso had said to her, how Mercedes had telegraphed messages across the room with her scissors. She especially wanted to ask Nelda why the more she tried not to think about Picasso, the more he seemed to be right there before her, grinning like he thought it was some kind of joke to keep invading somebody's thoughts. But Nelda was on her way to meet Eleanor, and Rowtina was on her own.

When eleven o'clock came, she bolted directly for Greenwich Avenue. There was an 11:20 showing of *Carmen Jones* at the Classic Regency. If anyone had told her six months ago that she'd be going to the movies alone in the middle of the night in Greenwich Village, she'd have laughed at how many parts of that picture were ridiculous. But tonight she was looking for a distraction—a big distraction. If only for a couple of hours.

Rowtina slid her cash under the window, bought herself a jumbo popcorn and a medium Diet Pepsi. She'd barely found her seat before the theater went dark and the screen was filled with soldiers, black soldiers. Rowtina thought, *Here I am in Greenwich Village at almost midnight in a theater filled with mostly white people watching an old movie about black people. Turtle, are you watching this? I know you'd have a mouthful to say.*

Then Dorothy Dandridge came onscreen, her shoulders shining and her hips outlined in a tight red skirt. Rowtina giggled. She tossed a few pieces of popcorn into her mouth and shook her head as if she had on the same silver gypsy earrings as Dorothy-Carmen. When Dorothy brazenly invited Harry Belafonte to a nightclub with his oatmeal faced sweetheart sitting right there in front of her, Rowtina was as dumbfounded as the sweetheart, but she couldn't imagine how Harry or any other man could refuse her.

Dorothy-Carmen unbuckled Army Boy Harry's belt as Harry tried to look unaroused, sucking on a peach. Rowtina felt someone lean in over her shoulder. He half whispered, "So, I don't look like Harry Belafonte. Who does? Is that why you won't let me take you dancing?"

Rowtina's Diet Pepsi went down the wrong way. Her throat ached so badly tears came to her eyes. She waited until she could swallow, turn, and manage to get out, "What are you doing here?"

"Am I not allowed to go to the movies now?" Picasso sounded vaguely indignant at the thought. "It's my neighborhood too, you know."

By now, Picasso's half-whisper had gotten very loud and one of the two men near Rowtina called to him, "I'd rather hear the movie, if you don't mind."

"May I sit with you?" Picasso asked her.

"No." Then she added, "Thank you."

Picasso headed down the aisle and sat, but not without looking back at her for what felt like a very long moment. At the same time, Dorothy-Carmen had caused Harry to knock his superior officer out cold because Harry was so jealous and crazy for her. Now they had to escape to Chicago.

It was hard for Rowtina not to be distracted with Picasso's head outlined in front of her by the light from the screen. When Dorothy-Carmen left Harry Belafonte locked up in a cheap hotel room to two-time him with the boxer Husky Miller, Rowtina was watching Harry and the top of Picasso's head simultaneously.

Pearl Bailey—Frankie, one of the barfly friends, cut a deck of cards to tell Dorothy-Carmen's fortune. "The cards don't lie," Pearl-Frankie warned her.

Dorothy-Carmen turned up Death, the nine of spades. "It ain't no use to run away from dat 'ol boy," she sang, "if he is chasing you."

Picasso's silhouette wasn't moving. Rowtina felt a chill go through her and it wasn't the air-conditioning in the theater.

Harry Belafonte followed Dorothy-Carmen to the big match where Husky Miller was boxing his championship bout. Husky won alright, but as Dorothy-Carmen left the fight, Harry caught up with her and dragged her into a storeroom under the stadium.

Rowtina kept one eye on Harry and the other on Picasso. She believed now that he had followed her—of course he had. This was no coincidence. He wanted her as much as Harry wanted Dorothy-Carmen and he'd follow her all over Greenwich Village if he had to, until she was his.

Dorothy-Carmen, in her strapless white cocktail dress, was getting the hellfire choked out of her. Sinking to the floor of that foul storeroom, she looked surprised. A man who not only looked like but was Harry Belafonte, a man who would blow her toenail polish dry and desert the army for her, was strangling her to death. Dorothy-Carmen had two-timed her last lover. By the time the military police got to the storeroom, Harry was crying over Dorothy-Carmen's beautiful, lifeless body. There was a blaze of fire against a black background on the screen and a choir sang.

Rowtina put her sweater around her shoulders, listening to the choir, watching the blaze. *Leave it to me to move down here to crazy-ass Greenwich Village and have some lunatic man following me, trying to kill me. Oh, Turtle, I've truly lost my mind.*

When there was a line of people between her and Picasso, she jumped up and started up the aisle, hoping he couldn't see her. She'd reached the theater exit when she heard him call out, "Now you're running from me?"

She stopped, trying to make her body look bold, unafraid, like Dorothy-Carmen's before she got her neck rung.

"Look," Picasso said, coming closer. "I will tell you my intentions. For tonight. I would like only to walk you to your door."

She turned to tell him no. Before she could, he said, "If not that, I could take you to your corner and I'll watch from there to see that you get into your building safely."

Picasso opened the theater door for Rowtina, and they both stepped outside. "Besides, it feels like rain." He held out his umbrella.

Rowtina remembered Lucy joking at a rainy Leave Him and Live meeting, "You can judge a man by the size of his umbrella. If he's got one of those twelve-inch, three-dollar collapsibles, don't expect any miracles in other areas. But a man totin' one of those old-fashioned three-foot suckers, wide enough for him to grab on to you under, that's a man who obviously knows what to do with a big piece of wood." Rowtina had refused to giggle along with the others that day at the meeting, but she heard Lucy's umbrella theory now as though Lucy was standing between her and Picasso, ranting it to all of Greenwich Village for the first time. Picasso had "one of those old-fashioned three-foot suckers." It was mushroom colored, like he was, with a thick, deep brown handle and a horse's head at the tip. Rowtina pulled her sweater up on her shoulders and muttered, "Maybe just to the corner, if you want."

As if on cue, it began to drizzle. Picasso immediately put up his umbrella and even more quickly, his arm was around her waist. Quick as an octopus, Rowtina thought. Then she pictured Harry Belafonte in his army uniform with a tentacle around her waist. "It ain't no use to run away from dat ol' boy, if he is chasing you."

Rowtina was Dorothy-Carmen in her white strapless gown. And here was Picasso–Harry Belafonte about to sneak his arm from her waist up to her throat and strangle her in the middle of Greenwich Village, where her white neighbors probably couldn't care less.

She suddenly felt compelled to blurt, "I was married, you know. I'm a widow. My husband, Turtle, only died this year." She knew she might have said "a few months ago" and didn't. He still might strangle her, but at least she'd go out having told him about Turtle.

"I'm very sorry."

Neither one of them said anything after that. For four blocks, Rowtina concentrated on Picasso's arm around her and could have sworn by the corner of Ninth that it was under her bra and inching upward. But she told herself she'd imagined it. *You've got to get inside quick, before you start talking in tongues or something, Rowtina. You've really gone over the cliff.*

"Well, this is my corner," she announced loud enough for people halfway down the block to hear.

"And I suppose you would prefer me to leave you here on the corner in the rain, rather than take you to your door."

"No. I was thinking that it seems to have let up some." People caught in the downpour without umbrellas raced in several directions in front of them. Picasso turned to Rowtina and laughed.

"But it hasn't." He was looking at her, she thought, as if he might be deciding finally that she was playing too hard at hard to get. But even so, he must not be thinking too harshly of her. "Look," he said gently, "I'm not sure exactly how far you have to go, but if you don't feel comfortable, why don't I give you my umbrella and I'll see if I can catch a cab?"

Before she could stop herself, it was out. "Why don't you walk me to my door? Then get yourself a cab." She'd never heard the voice before, come from herself, that is. And she couldn't begin to understand how she could sound so much like Dorothy Dandridge without even trying. But it was absolutely Dorothy-Carmen who'd said it. Picasso looked as stunned as Rowtina.

He continued down the block, without his arm around her this time. When they got to 57 Ninth Street, Rowtina put her hand on his arm. In that same tone, the one that sounded like bourbon and Lucky Strikes, Rowtina said, "I'll let you know about dinner."

She was trembling with shock and embarrassment. It wasn't at all how she'd intended to respond to him, if she'd been able to choose at all. Picasso's face showed that he was still shaken by her Jekyll and Hyde behavior, but he responded as though it was perfectly natural.

"Should I call you?"

Rowtina was afraid to say anything. She wasn't sure what would come out. Her eyes grew wide and her lips tightened.

Now Picasso was starting to look truly confused. "Or you could call me at the shop, when you decide. Either way. Whatever you'd like."

Rowtina nodded like her head was attached to a spring. She tried to smile at him at least, and she thought she succeeded.

Her key fought the outside lock as if she were a bumbling thief, trying to break in. Finally Picasso reached over, took it from her gently, and opened the door.

"Good night for now, Miss Rowtina Washington."

As she made her way to her new apartment, she heard something echoing behind her quite different from what she knew Picasso had said. She decided it was best to ignore it, keep going right into her apartment, and double-lock the door. But there it was again. As close as if he'd still had his arm around her waist, their hips moving against each other. Oh yessss, it most definitely was. Harry Belafonte. With a Spanish accent. Murmuring, "Good night for now, Miss Carmen Jones."

Fifteen

The next day, on the early shift, Rowtina muttered the same word continuously to herself as she admitted patients. "Possessed."

That was it, the only possible answer. Somehow, she'd fallen under the power of . . . what? *I should never have gone into that shop. And why didn't I get it when that Picasso said he didn't usually wash a customer's hair but he was going to wash mine. It didn't feel like any shampoo I've ever had. Who knows what he was really doing to me?* Rowtina studied her reflection in the emergency room window. *What I'll do is tell Nelda and Osceola the truth. I've been possessed. I don't know how exactly, but I have and I need their help.*

She got to the meeting room twenty minutes early, hoping she'd get a chance to speak to either Nelda, Osceola, or both. It was Nelda who came in first.

"I was waiting for you," Rowtina told her immediately. "I have to speak with you and Osceola after the meeting."

"What's the matter?"

Lucy and Aggie were coming in through the chapel. Rowtina had just enough time to blurt to Nelda, "Can the two of you please give me a few minutes after this is over? It's important."

"Osceola's going to want to know why you don't want to bring it up during the meeting," Nelda said.

By that time, Lucy and Aggie were already in the room. Rowtina thought, *I'm not trying to exclude them. I just feel closer to Osceola and Nelda.* She put on a false smile and murmured to Nelda, "Not this meeting. Alright?"

Lucy ran up to Rowtina to get a closer look. "What the hell did you do to yourself?"

"I got my hair cut," Rowtina said nervously. "Doesn't it look alright?"

"Look alright?" Lucy squealed. "Baby, you give me that number right now, you hear me? I want whatever they're sellin' and I want it now!"

"Lucy could use a whole lot more than a hairdressin' appointment," Aggie said. "If somebody don't calm that husband o' hers down real good, she's gonna need a plastic surgeon."

"What's going on, Lucy?" Nelda asked.

"There's nothin' new goin' on," Lucy answered. "Nothin' you don't already know."

But Aggie was bursting with it. "Sal's been botherin' Lucy like hell. He came into the Bun this morning and started carryin' on so bad some customers got up and walked out, and the ones who stayed were askin' Lucy if they should call the police. Then he left, but we kept seein' him across the street right up until an hour ago."

Nelda was stunned. "Where is he now? You should've called the police even after he was gone. Do you know where he is now?"

Lucy sighed, pulled her hair up in the back, and clipped it. "He's probably somewhere on his fifth beer braggin' about how he scared the shit out of his no-good tramp of a wife and now she'll think twice about stayin' away from their happy home."

Osceola scurried in chattering. "Aren't you all glad to have an early evening meeting? Nobody's on a late shift so we can all go out to dinner afterwards."

When she took in their faces, she couldn't tell who to ask what the trouble was. "What is it? What's happened?"

"It's Sal," Nelda began, but Aggie again couldn't wait to announce, "He came into the Bun this morning acting like a maniac."

Osceola turned to Lucy. "Did he hurt you?" When Lucy assured her he hadn't, Osceola insisted they start the meeting with a prayer before there was any further discussion. "We can go over all that sordidness once we've had a moment of meditation." She stood in the center of the room with both of her arms outstretched, her tiny head bowed, and her eyes closed. Rowtina smiled for a moment at the sight of Osceola's cranberry dyed hair and the small patch of scalp she could see shining through. *Maybe that'll be her solution to what's happening to me. She'll want us to pray for me to be unpossessed.*

The five of them—Nelda, Osceola, Rowtina, Lucy, and Aggie—held hands as Osceola said a special prayer of protection. "We know You're with us no matter who else is in the room," she intoned.

Rowtina looked up and saw a red-faced white man leering at them from the chapel next door. It didn't have to be Sal Antiglione. There were certainly lots of other white men in the hospital. Was it possible that Sal could be so crazy as to follow Lucy all the way up to the seventh floor to a room clearly marked RESERVED FOR EMPLOYEE USE ONLY? The greasy hair might have belonged to any number of patients, and so might the grayed stubble. It was the wide eyes cutting through the glass of the chapel window that told Rowtina whoever was staring at all of them was either a madman, a drunk, or both.

She gripped Osceola's hand tighter. Osceola stopped what she was saying about God caring for all the women in the world. She looked first at Rowtina to see if she'd taken ill or was in pain. Nelda and Aggie both opened their eyes to see what had happened. Only Lucy stood with her eyes still closed as if trusting that eventually Osceola would get her train of thought back and finish the prayer.

The man watched Lucy standing with her head bowed in reverence as though he'd never seen anything like it—as though those bloodshot eyes were seeing something so foreign, he was paralyzed by what he saw. For as soon as Lucy lifted her head and looked toward the window as if he'd called her by name, the chapel door flew open and he strode toward her. The spell had been broken.

"You prayin', huh? You better be prayin'!"

Lucy backed out of the circle, yelling, "What the hell do you think you're doin', Sal?! Why? Why can't you leave me alone?" Loud Lucy Antiglione with the gritty mouth sounded like an eight year old schoolgirl being bullied on a playground at recess.

Aggie and Nelda both moved toward her, like small defense tanks moving into position. Rowtina was frozen, trying to figure out if she should run through the chapel to the hall and call for help. They were trapped on the seventh floor with a big, drunken bear of a man who appeared to be getting bigger as he filled the room with the stench of beer and sweat.

Sal stopped moving when Aggie and Nelda joined Lucy. He looked as though he was contemplating whether to move forward or back. Before he could make up his mind, Osceola scurried over between him and the three women he was looming over. Now the women formed a diamond—Lucy furthest back, Nelda and Aggie on either side, and Osceola at the tip, directly in front of Sal Antiglione.

Osceola planted her feet wide like she could easily stretch out her arms and begin to pray again. Except that now her gaze was fixed on Sal Antiglione with a look that shocked and frightened Rowtina. Her palms, which had only moments ago clasped around Aggie's hand on one side and Lucy's on the other, were

now tiny gnarly fists. Her bony, oak brown knuckles jutted like razor blades. When she opened her mouth to speak, Rowtina heard the sounds that Osceola made but it was not conceivable that the words had come out of her body. "You take another step toward her, motherfucker, and I'll kill you myself."

Sal Antiglione looked as though Osceola had shot him. Or hit him with some heavy object that stunned him to the point of dazed stupor. He grinned stupidly. Then he nodded to Lucy, "So you got yourself a whole little nigger army here, don't ya?"

Osceola would have none of it. She leaned toward him like a tilted arrow. In the same voice, only deeper, she growled, "That's right. An army. And you got to go. Right now!"

His lips quivered slightly. One eye closed, then opened again. As if he were being dragged from behind, Sal Antiglione's mountainous frame backed toward the chapel door. When he could go no further, he lifted a hammy pink fist and shouted across the room to Lucy, "You prob'ly told them a pack o' lies about me, ya bitch!" And to the rest of the women he called out with a slight slur, "You believe what ya wanna believe. I'm a good man and a good husband. She's a big liar. She was a big liar the day I married her and she's been one every day since."

When he was gone, the women looked at one another. Then they all stared at Osceola. Lucy rushed over to her, wrapped her arms around the older woman, and lifted her off the ground. No one made a sound. Lucy had her face buried in Osceola's stomach when she said, "Thank you, Miss Osceola. Shit. I really thank you."

In a driving spring rain, they went to dinner at Just a Bite's to celebrate. Rowtina tried to persuade them to reconsider—she didn't want to be anywhere near Picasso's shop tonight. But the Sisterhood had had a triumph, and they wanted someplace familiar.

As they waited to be seated, Nelda whispered to Rowtina, "Do you still need to talk?"

Rowtina turned and nodded her head. "Absolutely. I have to."

Nelda nodded and Rowtina knew she'd find a way to let Osceola know. Two couples at the bar were singing along with Marvin Gaye and Tammi Terrell. Nelda teased Osceola, who was singing softly, too. "Don't think I don't hear you, Sister!" Rowtina saw her lean into Osceola and whisper something in her ear. Osceola looked at Rowtina and nodded. When they got to the back of the restaurant, Osceola eased into the booth next to Rowtina and patted her on the thigh as a signal. She continued her singing to "Ain't Nothin Like the Real Thing," pretending to be both Marvin and Tammi. The five of them laughed till Osceola was dabbing at tears.

Tonight, Osceola was wearing a peach colored dress with a cameo in the middle of her chest. At the center of the cameo was a silhouette of a woman with a long, angular face and wild locks. Rowtina complimented Osceola on it. The older woman placed her hand on the cameo gently. "From my Kara." Rowtina thought of her own mother's taste in jewelry, in everything, really. Sylvia Mention favored the traditional, what she called "classic." She would have appreciated that Osceola was wearing a cameo, but Rowtina could see her mother frowning on the silhouette's Medusa-like locks. Rowtina wondered if Kara had been there in the room with them when Osceola had challenged Sal Antiglione. She smiled, feeling certain that she had.

"We could order a nice big bottle of wine," Nelda suggested. "I know I could use a couple of glasses. What do you say? It's on me."

"No, it's on me," Lucy said. "I'm the one who should be buying. I've never seen a look like that on Sal's big mug since I've known him. The only thing I wish is that I had a picture of it."

"Lord," Aggie chimed in, "I think he was actually scared he

was gonna get his butt beat by five women, startin' with Miss Osceola."

When the wine came, Lucy made a toast. "To Miss Osceola and Nelda, Rowtina and Aggie. God bless ya. May the circle be unbroke."

As the Sisterhood rehashed the details of the encounter with Sal Antiglione, Rowtina rehearsed what she'd say to Nelda and Osceola. Would Osceola be able to help her stand up to whatever was trying to overtake her, like she'd done for Lucy? Rowtina took a sip of her wine and looked over at Osceola. *Come on, Miss Osceola. Work a miracle for me too.*

They left the restaurant with Nelda carefully making it clear she was exhausted from all the excitement. "We're going to put Osceola in a cab uptown and then you and I are going to walk home together, Rowtina. Is that alright with you two?"

Rowtina and Osceola agreed. Lucy reluctantly agreed to go home with Aggie, mostly because Aggie said it would keep her from having a fight with her husband about getting home late. All of them made Lucy promise to call the police if there was any sign of Sal.

After Aggie and Lucy turned the corner, Nelda, Osceola, and Rowtina headed toward Rowtina's apartment. Nelda asked, "You want to start now, Rowtina, or should we wait till we get inside?"

"It can wait," Rowtina answered. With all her preparation, she was nervous now. What if it all sounded foolish, especially compared to what had happened with Lucy? Once they were in the apartment, though, she would have felt more foolish had she not tried to explain and see what they said.

The women tossed their umbrellas in Rowtina's bathtub and proceeded into the living room. Nelda took off her shoes and folded herself into the couch. "You got any of that hootch I told you to stash away?"

Rowtina was embarrassed. She wouldn't have wanted Osceola to know she kept liquor in the house. But her own mother had suggested, when Rowtina admitted to her how she wasn't exactly sleeping through the night, that she buy a half-pint of brandy. "Put a little shot in some tea, or warm milk, even. It's against my religion to lose sleep over anything or anybody." Sylvia Mention informed her, but added a warning. "Just don't ever get too comfortable running in and out of liquor stores."

Rowtina had chosen to stay awake until almost dawn waiting for Turtle rather than use the brandy as a sedative. Nelda saw the sealed bottle the day Rowtina moved and teased her, "You better give me that expensive brandy, girl. You're probably using it as a bookend." But when Rowtina actually offered it to her, Nelda refused. "It never hurts to have a little hootch on the premises."

Now Nelda was asking her if she had it in front of Osceola. She told Nelda weakly, "Yes, I still have the brandy. I haven't opened it, though. Should I make drinks for you two?"

"Naw," Nelda told her, "I was thinking maybe you needed it." Rowtina shook her head no.

"Let's get down to business," Osceola said. She sat in one corner of the couch, Nelda was in the other. Rowtina sat across from the two of them with the coffee table in between. She thought, *I don't have to tell it all. There's no reason I can't pick and choose exactly what I say.*

She began slowly and cautiously, starting with her first encounter with Picasso. She described Mercedes and how she suspected Picasso had not been entirely honest about their relationship. By the time she finished telling how she'd agreed to let Picasso walk her home from the movies and then surprised herself by flirting with him about going to dinner, she didn't know whether she felt more relieved or ashamed. But she hadn't left anything out.

Nelda, for once, said nothing. She stared at Osceola as though she were an African priestess oracle she'd led Rowtina on a pilgrimage to.

"My, things have certainly gotten involved since the day we stopped outside the salon," Osceola said, but there didn't seem to be any judgment in her eyes. She didn't, as Nelda predicted she might, urge Rowtina to bring it up at a Leave Him and Live meeting for a group consensus.

Instead, she leaned over and put both hands on the table with her fingers spread wide. She tilted her head back slowly, looking up at the ceiling as if she were having a vision. "Harry Belafonte and Dorothy Dandridge," she purred. "Those two were dangerous together then and they're dangerous together now, aren't they?"

Rowtina nodded.

"And they were all you needed, considering you were feeling hoodooed anyway. Huh?"

Rowtina laughed. The idea of it was both funny and strangely accurate—but odd, she thought, coming from Osceola. "All I know is that I can't stop thinking about this man. And the thoughts I'm having are . . ."

"We know what they are," Nelda said. "They're telling you you're alive."

Rowtina ignored her and directed her question to Osceola. "What do you think I should do?"

"Only one thing to do," Osceola proclaimed without hesitation. "You've got to fight fire with fire."

Rowtina folded her hands in her lap and crossed her ankles. "You mean, stay away from Picasso."

"I'm not telling you to stay away from anybody. Not my place—although it might be the safest thing to do, considering

what you say about this Mercedes woman. No, I'm suggesting
you might need what they call a consciousness cleanser. Vacuum
it out. Lift it a bit."

Nelda and Rowtina both leaned in closer as Osceola spread
her fingers even wider.

"Higher Plane Tea."

"I beg your pardon."

"Higher Plane Tea," Osceola repeated. "I think it will help.
And it obviously couldn't hurt."

"What is it?" Rowtina asked.

"Exactly what I said. A good cleanser. Seems to me you got a
fever rummaging around inside you, and from what you say, it's
rummaging pretty deep. So, I'm suggesting a treatment. All natural. You got a pen?"

Rowtina started to search, but Nelda reached into her bag
and pulled out a gold-plated one with her initials on it. "Here."

Osceola clasped her hands in front of her and instructed
Rowtina like a seasoned physician. "You go to any reasonably
stocked health food store. They got one around here, Nelda?"

"Yes. Over on Thirteenth. The Good Earth. They'll charge
you a month's rent for a head of lettuce, but the store's about a
half a block long. I'd be real surprised if they didn't have whatever she'll need."

Osceola nodded and told Rowtina, "You're only going to need
a little of each ingredient, cause it's a pretty potent tea. I'd tell
you I'd take the rest off your hands, but it's been quite a while
since I've needed this particular blend, thank God."

Nelda hooted. "I've seen you sizing up Dr. Benjamin and Dr.
Marshall, too, Miss Osceola. You can't tell me any different."

But Osceola would barely allow her mouth a smile. "You
might have seen me looking. And I'm glad to still be able. But
I'm not fixated. That's the difference. Yes?"

Her two younger companions agreed sheepishly.

"Now, it's a thimble full of cayenne, half of a jack-in-the-pulpit root—sometimes that's a little difficult, depending on where you go—a quarter of a collinsonia root, one bay leaf, and a quarter of a cup of minced goldenseal root. Make sure you get the root, not the powder."

Rowtina stopped writing and looked up. "Is that it?"

Osceola shook her head. "No. And I want you to listen especially careful to this part, because this is the most important. There's a tiny shop in Chinatown. It's nothing but a hole in the wall, a half block south of Canal, east side of the street. Green Tea, that's the name of it. You go to Green Tea and ask for three ounces of essence of pussywillow. Shouldn't cost you more than nine or ten dollars. And that is your vital ingredient. Mind you, use no more, no less. Boil everything else together for ten to twelve minutes at best. You don't want to boil off the potency of the herbs. Then, while your tea is steeping, add your pussywillow."

"And do I only drink it once?" Rowtina was trying to be polite, but she couldn't help thinking, *How can Osceola be serious about this? And Nelda, has she heard this before?*

"We'll see. Everybody's system is different. And only you will really know how it takes effect."

"Have you tried Higher Plane, Nelda?" Rowtina ventured.

"Never had the occasion." Nelda was brisk but respectful.

"Well, I'm going to get my ingredients tomorrow." Rowtina tried to sound confident and grateful.

"You let me know when you boil up your tea," Nelda chuckled. "I want to come down and watch it smoke up blue and shoot sparks."

Osceola didn't seem to mind Nelda's teasing. She put her head back against Rowtina's couch and closed her eyes. "Make sure you do everything exactly like I told you, Rowtina Washington. If you don't," she smiled, "blue smoke and sparks are a definite possibility."

Sixteen

The only thing more humiliating than being in this situation is not having the good sense to keep it to myself.

Rowtina awoke embarrassed at everything she'd told Nelda and Osceola the night before. When the phone rang, she thought she might have a chance to tell at least one of them she'd exaggerated the whole thing.

"Hello?"

"I thought I'd come downtown and see what you've gotten yourself into."

Rowtina panicked. *What on earth is happening?* "Good morning, Mama. What do you mean 'what I've gotten myself into'?"

"I mean, I thought I'd come down and see your Greenwich Village apartment. I could wait for an invitation, but I'm an old woman. I might not be able to walk on my own by the time I received it."

Rowtina laughed, mostly out of relief. She couldn't have imagined how Sylvia Mention would know what she'd really gotten herself into. "Of course you're invited, Mama. You're always invited. Are you coming today?"

"Is it a bad time?"

"No, it's not a bad time. I don't go into work until later. I was going to do some shopping, but it can wait."

"It doesn't have to wait. I don't mind going shopping. As long as I get to see where you live before I come back uptown."

Rowtina pictured Sylvia Mention traveling with her to Chinatown to the Green Tea shop to purchase three ounces of pussywillow. "Really, Mama. Shopping can wait. Do you want me to come up and get you?"

"No, I certainly do not. Don't be insulting. Do you really think I need you to escort me down to the Village? I was going to the Village before you were born. I will be down there in about an hour. Is that alright?"

Rowtina scowled at the phone but answered quietly, "Of course it's alright, Mama. Why don't I meet you at the train then? I'll be right outside the station when you get off at Fourteenth Street."

"Very well. But I'm also quite capable of coming directly to your home."

"I know. But I'll meet you at the train. It's nine-thirty now. I'll be at the Fourteenth Street stop at ten-thirty, and I'll wait until you get there."

"Is there anything you need me to bring?"

"No Mama, nothing. I'll see you soon."

Rowtina hung up, studying the phone as though waiting for her mother to have her usual last word. *Leave it to her. By ten-thirty I expected to be on my way to Chinatown. Instead, I'll be wasting my breath trying to convince her that I'm fine, I've made the right decision and no, I won't be moving back uptown come the first of the month.*

Taking a quick inventory of the apartment, she decided, *I'll run to The Good Earth now and buy the rest of the ingredients. On the way back, I'll go to the station and pick Mama up. After she leaves, I'll take the train down to Chinatown and get the pussywillow.*

*   *   *

Shopping for the roots, Rowtina began to think about Picasso again. She scolded herself for picturing him and trying to fill in details, remembering the way he smelled and how his hands felt on her temples and the nape of her neck.

She put the bag from Good Earth very carefully at the bottom of the large leather satchel she'd brought with her. Then she placed her light sweater on top of it. Camouflage. Even if Sylvia Mention happened to glance in, all she'd see was the sweater.

At 10:15, she was a block away from the subway station when she happened to casually put her hand to her hair. Since the moment she'd left Picasso's salon, she'd been enjoying how all the different woolly, wavy, baby-fine textures of it felt.

"Oh my God," she gasped. Sylvia Mention had not seen her hair, nor had Rowtina prepared her for it. "She'll go crazy. She'll take one look at it and go out of her mind."

Rowtina looked up and down Fourteenth Street at the dozens of small shops filled with cheap articles of clothing, shoes, jewelry, and wigs. Several feet away was a store with huge bins of women's clothing on the street in front of it. Quickly scanning the bins, Rowtina kept moving into the store, where more of the merchandise was heaped, until she saw a sign over several baskets proclaiming, "LADEEZ 100% SILK DESIGINAR SCARFES—3 FOR $10!!!"

She rushed over and began to sort through the layers of loud squares of shiny fabric—brightly patterned with triangles, polka dots, and animal prints. Rowtina remembered all too well what her mother thought about animal prints. Sylvia Mention said if you didn't own the real thing—mink stole, leopard coat, zebra cape—you shouldn't wear cheap imitations. "Only thing worse than cheap imitation animal skin is cheap imitation animal prints," she declared. "Only poor people with bad taste wear cheap imitation animal anything." But there was something about both the zebra and the leopard she was attracted to. And if

she was going to take advantage of the bargain, it might as well
be something she liked.

Rowtina selected a tan colored scarf with dark brown stitch-
ing around the edge that she didn't particularly care for and the
leopard and zebra print scarves. She went further into the store
and handed the woman behind the counter a ten-dollar bill.

"For so cheap, you should get three more," the woman
advised, flashing several gold rimmed teeth.

"I'll come back," Rowtina told her. She folded the tan scarf
into a triangle and covered her hair with it.

"It's a pretty scarf, but your hair is prettier."

Rowtina smiled up at the woman behind the counter.
"Thanks."

Waiting inside the subway station, Rowtina peered through
the iron bars and down the stairs at the platform. When a train
approached, she adjusted her scarf, checking to make sure her
hair could not be seen. Rowtina saw Sylvia Mention get off the
downtown express and stand, looking up and down the platform,
trying to choose an exit. "Mama, I'm up here," she called, surprising herself at how much like a small child she sounded, so
pleased to see her mother coming toward her.

Sylvia Mention did not acknowledge her until she reached
the top of the stairs. "It's so warm," she said. "And not a breath
of air to be had on that train. Why do you have on that scarf?
How can you stand it?"

"My hair. I didn't have time to do anything to it. Ran right out
after you called." Rowtina smiled at her nervously. "I thought
we'd go to the apartment first. You could rest and I could fix you
some lunch."

"It's not even eleven o'clock in the morning. What would I
need to rest from? Riding the subway? Why don't we do your

shopping like we said and then we can take the groceries back to your apartment?"

"I told you, Mama. I'm not going to waste time shopping when you've come downtown to visit me. I can go shopping anytime. Let's go to the apartment. I want you to see it. You'll like it. You'll be proud of me."

Sylvia Mention was silent as they walked back to Ninth Street. Rowtina pointed out Mount Olive as they passed it, exclaiming, "Wait till you see how close it is to the house. I can leave my apartment and be at work in less than fifteen minutes. No more taking the train at eleven o'clock at night. I punch out, walk through the hospital doors, and before I know it, I'm home!" Sylvia Mention studied her daughter's face.

When they got to her building, Rowtina reached into her bag, nervously digging between the other new scarves and the herbs from The Good Earth. She pulled out her keys and immediately dropped them. "Why are you so shaky?" Sylvia Mention wanted to know. "You back on coffee?"

"No, I'm not back on coffee. I'm excited, that's all. I didn't think you'd want to come to my apartment."

Rowtina opened the door and Sylvia Mention stepped inside. Barely past the threshold, she stared across the room. "What is that?"

"It's a copy of a famous painting called *Susannah in Harlem.*" Rowtina put her bag down on the couch and hoped that could be the end of the explanation. She'd forgotten to consider what her mother might think of the print.

"Is that where you bought it? In Harlem? I don't remember seeing anything like that up there."

"No. Some friends gave it to me as a housewarming gift."

"What friends?" her mother asked.

Rowtina knew better than to introduce the idea of the Sisterhood to her mother. "They're from the hospital."

"Those women who were at the church? The ones who brought liquor to your husband's funeral?"

"They were trying to help." Rowtina tried to think of a distraction, anything that would take the conversation in a different direction.

Sylvia Mention stared from *Susannah in Harlem* bathing in her tub back to Rowtina. She still hadn't taken one more step into the apartment. "Rowtina, why do you still have that thing tied around your head?"

"I'm embarrassed, Mama. I told you, I didn't have time to do anything to my hair."

"Well, I want to see what shape it's in. Have you let it go, down here where nobody would know how to take care of it?"

"Mama, my hair is fine."

Sylvia Mention was losing her patience. "Rowtina, take off that scarf. I want to see your hair."

Rowtina sighed, reached up, and slowly pulled the scarf back. Sylvia Mention let out an anguished moan as though she'd been kicked in the groin. "I knew it. I knew it the minute I saw you. And you lied."

"I was trying not to spoil our visit."

"It was spoiled the moment you let someone make a fool out of you like that. And you didn't think I'd know? Were you going to wear that cheap, ugly scarf the whole time I was here?"

Rowtina couldn't think of anything to say or do, except stay perfectly still like a small animal in the face of danger.

"What the hell is going on down here?" her mother demanded of her. "First, you move away from everything you were raised to be. You cut your hair as short and nappy as any man's, and you tell me the same women who brought liquor to your husband's funeral are now buying you paintings of naked Susannahs to hang in your new Greenwich Village apartment. Sweet Jesus, tell me what is going on?"

Rowtina shook her head from side to side as though stirring up the words before she could get them out. "Nothing, Mama. Nothing is going on."

"No, something is most definitely going on. But I'll tell you this—you may be turning into something totally different than the girl I thought I raised, but I'm still exactly who I've always been. And I don't like your naked woman paintings, I don't like the butcher job you let somebody do on your hair, and I can only pray that whatever you're going through has a time limit. Maybe when the time is up, you'll regain your senses and come back uptown to your own people."

They stood in silence. And because she had hope that something of their morning together might be salvaged, Rowtina said, "I could get you a cup of tea, Mama, if you'd like."

"I don't think so," Sylvia Mention answered quietly. "I came down to see where you live and now I've seen it. I'm going to go on back uptown and let you get to your shopping."

Rowtina walked closer to where her mother was standing. She wanted to touch her.

"I wish you'd stay a little longer," Rowtina said.

"No. Not today. You take care of your business. I'm going home."

They left the apartment and walked to the subway together without a word passing between them. At the subway entrance, Rowtina stopped, again wanting so much to reach for her mother. And this time she did. Sylvia Mention stood erect and motionless, allowing herself to be hugged. When Rowtina pulled away, her mother was staring at her hair.

Rowtina wanted to tell her, "Everyone I know likes it," but she knew it would probably sound as foolish as it felt. "I'll call to see if you got home alright," she said.

"At eleven o' clock in the morning? Rowtina, please. Go do your shopping."

Sylvia Mention went down the stairs to the train as Rowtina watched. It reminded her of watching Turtle as he'd disappeared down another flight of stairs. "Bye, Mama," she called. And, as Turtle had not acknowledged her call, neither did her mother. When the train pulled out of the Fourteenth Street station, Rowtina ran her hands over her hair and sighed.

Seventeen

Rowtina had no trouble finding the Green Tea shop, but Dr. Cheng, the owner and practitioner, wasn't there. Precise in her request for "three ounces of essence of pussywillow, no more, no less," Rowtina was irritated when the curt old woman tending the store overpoured the finely ground silver powder. Rowtina expected she'd ask her for more than the nine or ten dollars Osceola had told her it should cost. But the crone spat out "ten" as she slid the small paper bag of powder toward Rowtina and scrutinized her for the first time, waiting to be paid.

Once she got home with her packages, Rowtina suspected she might run into Nelda in the apartment building. What she found instead was a message on her answering machine. "I would never disrespect Miss Osceola by acting like I didn't believe in something she was saying, but I wouldn't blame you and I definitely wouldn't snitch if you didn't go out and buy those ingredients." There was a brief silence before the message continued, "But if you do, I definitely want to be there when you mix 'em and throw 'em back."

When Rowtina left again for work, she laughed to herself, thinking, *I bet Nelda calls downstairs to the emergency room and asks me if we can walk home together so she can watch me drink my tea, smoke up blue, and shoot sparks.*

But Nelda didn't call or leave another message. Eleven

o'clock came and Rowtina punched out at the end of her shift. She half expected she'd be coming back to work the next day so changed a woman that everyone in the hospital would notice. Walking home, she glanced from the corner down the block to the Classic Regency, where *Carmen Jones* had been playing only a few nights before. The marquee had been changed. There was no sign of Dorothy or Harry. They had only been there one night, as if by hoodoo, as Osceola had put it. Now they were gone. Or were they? Maybe they'd moved right off the screen and followed Rowtina home. Maybe they were both there now, waiting in her apartment, placing bets with each other on whether Osceola's Higher Plane Tea could do what she claimed it could.

Rowtina didn't dare look down Tenth Street. She was concentrating hard. She didn't want to see the salon, and she absolutely didn't want to see Picasso. *I'm going to lift my consciousness, like Osceola said. Cleanse it.*

This is my contribution, the part I can add. She pulled the lavender gown edged in satin from the bureau. She hadn't worn it in months, since the night she'd thought how much Turtle would appreciate it and he hadn't shown up. That was supposed to be a night she'd want to celebrate. Instead, Turtle had let her down.

But tonight, tonight was as much for Turtle as it was for her. Even though she hadn't actually done anything wrong, it was entirely possible Turtle might think he had reason not to trust her. But by morning, he'd have to know that she was back to the same Rowtina he knew, his Rowtina.

The gown didn't fit quite the same as it had a few months ago. Rowtina seemed to fill out the bosom a little more than she remembered. *And will you look at what's happened to my behind? I've never had a behind like this. It looks like a horse's butt with a couple yards of nylon thrown over it.* But the more she looked at herself in the gown, the more appealing she thought she looked, from bosoms to backside.

Rowtina put her mixture of cayenne (she actually used a thimble to measure it), jack-in-the-pulpit root, collinsonia, bay leaf, and minced goldenseal into a saucepan, barely covered it with water, and lit a fire under it. She went back into the bedroom to take another look at herself, dabbed her wrists, the insides of her elbows, and between her breasts with Dusk and Diamonds. She'd stopped long enough to buy the perfume at a fancy drugstore on her way home from work because she'd seen the ad in Dina's *Vanity Fair* magazine. There was something about the couple half naked in the sand under the palm tree that made her think of places she'd never been. And when she smelled it in the store, well, it was certainly a perfume she wasn't sure she'd ever get up enough courage to wear out anywhere, but now, in her gown, looking like she did . . . Rowtina wondered for a moment if the perfume would interfere with the power of the tea. But how could it? *One's going on the outside, the other on the inside. There can't be any problem if they're not going to mix.*

Rowtina went back to the kitchen to check on the Higher Plane. She remembered Osceola's warning not to let the boiling exceed ten to twelve minutes lest the potency of the herbs be lost. Picking up the tiny paper bag containing the essence of pussywillow, Rowtina pictured the old woman overpouring the powder. She was certain that it exceeded the three ounces "no more, no less" Osceola had stipulated. She shrugged. *I'll just have to trust that a little more is better than a little less.*

The combination of the powder and herbs in the boiled water smelled like spoiled food. Osceola hadn't said it would smell bad. Rowtina held her breath and poured. She took her cup and went into the living room. Determined to enjoy the promise of a spiritual cleansing, Rowtina put on a Cassandra Wilson CD.

"She's as sweet as tupelo honey

"She's an angel of the first degree"

Nelda had introduced Rowtina to Cassandra's music, shocked that she'd never heard of the singer before. Rowtina admired Cassandra's wild looking hair; the sound of her voice made her wish she was a jazz singer. Catching a reflection of herself in the mirror, she laughed. It was the laugh she hadn't heard come out of herself until she'd gone to see *Carmen Jones*. If she were a jazz singer, she'd wear dresses exactly like this lavender nightgown and perform in front of hundreds of people in them. She'd pretend they absolutely were for the stage and that she knew damn well what she was doing when she put them on.

Rowtina glided into the bedroom, anticipating her first sip of Higher Plane. She sat up on her bed with her legs spread, making herself more comfortable, and drank. *Ugh! Good Lord, this is foul! Osceola didn't tell me it would taste like this. How on earth can I drink this?*

Rivulets of perspiration ran between her breasts, from her armpits, between her thighs. The consistency of the tea was so thick that it made her feel even fuller. But she continued to sip. She fanned herself and lifted her gown above her thighs. *I'll tell you one thing. These are more than "decently shaped" legs, Mama. These are damned good legs.* She ran her finger up the back of one of them, pretending she was straightening a seam, like Dorothy Dandridge had done. *My seams straight, soldier?*

Easing her hands up her gown to her breasts, touching her nipples, she thought of a word she'd read in Dina's *Vanity Fair* describing the young Sophia Loren. "Voluptuous." *Vol up tu ous. That's what I am. I don't know when it happened. But I am.* She gently squeezed her breasts, pinched her nipples until they stung. Vol up tu ous. She took another sip of tea and ran her hand across the back of her damp neck. *This is the most horrible tasting mess . . . Higher Plane indeed!*

She set her cup down on the nightstand and ran into the

kitchen to the cupboard—pushed aside her bottles of olive oil, safflower oil, balsamic vinegar. Behind them all, there it was— where she'd hidden it in a corner—the half-pint of brandy. She took a knife from the cupboard drawer and cut the seal. *I can't take another swallow of this Higher Plane concoction without something in it to change the taste. I'll pretend it's one of those mixed drinks with the fancy names Nelda orders that she says I should try.*

She'd be the jazz singer with wild red curls in a lavender gown, after a set. "I'll have a Plane, please, with a healthy shot of brandy and a double dose of pussywillow." Rowtina put her wrist to her nose to smell her Dusk and Diamonds. Then she took a good gulp of this new cocktail she'd mixed. She thought she was going to be very sick for a moment, but it passed. Beginning to perspire again, she was the jazz singer, flushed with the heat of herself. Across the room wasn't Rowtina's kitchen, but the elegant room where the jazz singer sang for men in silk suits and women wearing chic black dresses. Even in a room as crowded as this, it was easy to spot him. His own blue silk jacket hung open over a starched white shirt with covered buttons. His pants hung so she could see the muscles in his thighs, and his eyes told her that he hadn't minded, but he had indeed been waiting for her.

With a slight nod, she sent him a message. "Follow me." When she got into the bedroom, she turned on the light next to her bed. She wanted there to be light. She wanted to see him and for him to see her.

Sitting on the bed, Rowtina took several more swallows of her cocktail and placed it on the night table. She eased down onto the bed, waiting. *I don't know what I'm supposed to be feeling, but I know I feel good. Not entirely like myself, but whoever it is, she's not complaining either. This Higher Plane needed a little help, that's all. I wish I could tell Osceola, cause it definitely would make her recipe taste a whole lot better.*

There was a long, harsh wail of a horn in the street. For an instant, Rowtina panicked. *Turtle. Oh my God, maybe it's Turtle.* She closed her eyes tightly, trying to stop from feeling so warm, so moist everywhere. She reached to push her gown down. *What the hell are you doing, Rowtina?* She listened. *If it's you, you've got to come in right now and let me see you. I need you right now.* Silence. It wasn't Turtle. Maybe Turtle was never going to come to her again.

Her palms brushed her belly, moved further into the folds of her gown, until they began to do what they wanted, kneading and searching, and she didn't stop them. It was entirely possible Turtle was never going to come to her again.

She didn't dare open her eyes. The man in the silk suit had followed her in from the other room. He was kneeling over her now, she could smell him. It was his hair brushing past her breasts that announced who he was and what he was hungry for. His words were muffled, but she understood the accent, the lovely way his tongue curled around the *R* in "Rowtina," making it sound new. She wouldn't sing again tonight for anyone but him, as she held on to his tight, coarse curls. She'd sing and sigh and buck and flow sweet, sweet tupelo honey.

Eighteen

There were fourteen exactly. When Rowtina first saw them the next morning lying on her doormat—the doormat Turtle bought when they moved into the brownstone as newlyweds—she thought there were a dozen. But when she stooped to pick them up, searching for a card or a message of some kind, she realized there had to be more. Outside her apartment, on her knees, she counted. Eleven, twelve, thirteen, fourteen. Fourteen roses, pink and red mixed together. As delicately tight and curled closed as sleeping babies' lips. When she finally stood up and pushed her nose deep into the bouquet, she saw the card and pulled it out. "Thank you for letting me walk you home."

When exactly had he brought them? Had he followed her from the hospital? Had a neighbor let him in, or taken the flowers from him and left them, maybe minutes ago, on the mat? They couldn't have been there that long—this was New York City. Rowtina didn't know all her neighbors, but there weren't any she'd seen she didn't think capable of stealing a big bouquet of roses from outside someone else's door.

Propelled. Both pushed and pulled, and at a speed that left her breathless. By whom or what, she didn't know, and she didn't particularly care. She hurried down Ninth Street, constantly glancing into shop windows at her reflection. Last night, she'd had deep, burgundy locks. This morning, she patted in place the sleek, close-cropped haircut Picasso had given her. He'd told her more than once that he thought her hair was perfect. This morning, it looked like he might not be far from wrong.

Turning the corner onto Tenth Street, it seemed the only building on the block was Picasso's Salon de Belleza. The small potted trees framing the door looked like their buds might sprout blossoms by the time she reached them. When she went in, she couldn't remember how she got from the street to the front desk, and again, it didn't matter.

Christine, the receptionist, was mincing toward her in head to toe tangerine, like an early summer elf. Lurking at her post, Mercedes definitely hadn't missed Rowtina coming into the salon. Mercedes was wearing a short black jumper and very high pumps. Her flaming hair seemed bigger than ever, a sorceress's headdress of scarlet feathers. She said something that caused the other two hairdressers to cackle loudly. But Picasso was striding toward Rowtina, beaming. "You are here!" he called, and she felt like royalty landing. "Come," he said, pulling her toward the back of the shop.

She was gliding, practically flying behind him. When she stopped, before Picasso could say anything else, Rowtina announced to him, "I've come to invite you to dinner. At my apartment."

Yes, it did sound eerily like someone else had said it. Of course it did. But by now, Rowtina was used to sounding like different women at different times. It was tremendous, actually, this surge of strange but ecstatic energy. And as long as it felt this good, who was Rowtina Washington to question it?

"Are you sure?" Picasso asked.

"Yes," she said without hesitation. "Saturday night. Would that be alright?"

"It would be much more than alright."

"I want to make you something you'll like. I don't know much about Spanish food."

"Then maybe I should cook for you. There are several Mexican dishes you might like."

"Mexican?"

"Ah, so you are surprised. Everyone thinks if you are Spanish and living in New York, you are undoubtedly Puerto Rican. But yes, I am Mexican."

"I'm not surprised at all," she lied quickly. "I was trying to think if I knew any Mexican dishes at all."

"In that case, please do not worry. Whatever pleases you I'm sure will please me."

"Seven o'clock, then," she instructed him. Then she added, "Thank you so much for the roses."

Picasso nodded and smiled. "I'll see you on Saturday."

She lifted her head high and started out, certain that every woman in the shop had heard their conversation. They were all staring at her, she decided, and it thrilled her. What she saw in the mirror, though, caused her to stop dead.

There, seated in none other than Mercedes's chair, was Lucy Antiglione, grinning at her with those enormous new teeth as though she'd just hatched six porcelain eggs and was holding them in her mouth.

"Rowtina! Damn! I should have known! And how long has Picasso been doing your hair, darlin'?!"

Rowtina allowed herself to be caught off-guard only for an instant. Mercedes stood right behind Lucy, her comb caught in midair. Rowtina knew she had no choice but to answer both of them.

"I've only been here once before," she said briskly, trying to sound nonchalant.

Mercedes snorted and snapped the comb down on her counter. "She's one of Picasso's newest customers. What did he do to you today, and so quickly too?"

Rowtina's lips widened in a defiant smile, almost without her meaning to. "Oh, I came on personal business today." And with absolute glee she added, "Strictly personal."

Mercedes began to comb poor Lucy's limp, stringy hair as if she was hoeing gravel. Lucy wailed, "Owwww!"

Rowtina waved, "See ya later!" at the two of them and purposely left the salon door open behind her.

There was no doubt about it. She was strutting. She'd never strutted in her life, nor would she have thought her hips, pelvis, or chest were capable. But here she was, most definitely strutting down Tenth Street.

Mexican. Isn't that something? I guess I really didn't consider that he was anything but Puerto Rican and I'm not even sure I was thinking much about that. Why should I have? The only thing I was thinking was that I'm having a friend over for dinner. Doesn't matter what he looks like or where he's from. I'll make a nice Mexican dinner for him. And get to know him better. That's Christian friendship. Extending your hand. Getting to know your neighbor.

She imagined herself, Rowtina Washington, born and raised a black woman in Harlem, New York, preparing and serving an astonishing Mexican meal to an astounded and grateful Picasso Alegria.

The only thing dimming that brilliant image was a disturbing vision of Lucy Antiglione amply filling Mercedes Moreno's salon chair. How in the world had that happened?

Nineteen

"Yes, of course I drank it! I told you I did."

"Did you follow Osceola's instructions and measure everything out?"

"Nelda, I did everything I was supposed to do. The woman who sold me the essence of pussywillow might have miscalculated a little, but I did exactly as Osceola told me to." Mentioning the brandy was out of the question. Rowtina was sure of it.

"Well, you sure sound like you're not saying everything. Is it because you're busy down there? We could meet when you take your break. How do you feel? Do you feel a difference?"

"Oh yes. I definitely feel different. I couldn't even begin to describe how different."

"And what about the hairdresser? Have you seen him?"

"Nope. Haven't seen him." *Please God, don't let me tell any more lies to Nelda.* "Listen, Nelda, you're right. We're so busy down here tonight, I feel guilty being on the phone. *Whoops, there goes another one.* "We can talk tomorrow at the meeting. Alright?"

"Okay, but I still say you sound funny. You've got me a little worried, baby girl."

"Don't be. Please. Gotta go. Night-night, Nelda."

Rowtina hung up feeling guilty yet relieved. "Dina?"

At the other end of the counter, Dina Tamaris was picking pepperoni off a slice of pizza.

"Do I look any different to you from, let's say, last night?"

"Rowtina," Dina said calmly, "I don't try to keep up with you anymore. You've seemed different every half hour for the past few months."

Rowtina sighed and smiled. *I probably have. And sometimes, in less time than that.*

On Friday afternoon, Rowtina was still dodging both Nelda and Osceola. She hadn't figured out yet what to say to them about the effects of her own blend of Higher Plane Tea. She was also not especially eager to see Lucy.

But there was a meeting, and Rowtina reluctantly made her way up to Mount Olive's seventh floor. From the moment she saw Lucy's hair, she was confused. It looked exactly as it always did—certainly no less limp, straggly, or gray. Apparently, she'd made an appointment, gotten as far as Mercedes's chair, and not even gotten a decent dye job.

They all joined hands for a short prayer. Rowtina tried not to think Osceola was hinting anything when she prayed, "Let all of us feel that we can come into the circle with the truth about any situation and without fear of judgment."

The women had barely sat down when there was a loud clickety-clicking through the chapel. The door opened and Mercedes Moreno, in a tight chartreuse blouse and matching stretch pants, strolled in and stood in front of all of them, beaming at Lucy. Rowtina stared in disbelief.

Osceola greeted her warmly, but sounding a little unsure. "Hello. May I help you?"

Lucy stood up as though she'd sat on a sewing needle. "This is Mercedes. I told her about us." She looked at Rowtina blankly. "She was very interested in our meetings."

Mercedes smiled brightly at Rowtina, tossed her hair, and assumed the familiar beauty contestant stance next to Lucy. Rowtina braced herself for whatever might be next.

"You're Mercedes?" Osceola repeated.

"Mercedes Moreno."

Mercedes spoke in a clear accented voice with a slight tremor in it. "I'm so happy to be here. If my good friend Lucy had not told me of this place where other women would understand what I'm going through, I am afraid to think what I might have done next."

Lucy Antiglione choked out a cigarette cough that sounded like someone was strangling her. Or about to.

Osceola reached for an empty folding chair. "Please sit down. We're happy to have you with us, Mercedes." Aggie rushed to place the chair in front of Mercedes. "I'm Osceola and this is Nelda, Aggie, and Rowtina."

Mercedes maintained her sad smile as she focused on each face. When she got to Rowtina, she paused for a moment. "Hello to you all and thank you for making me feel welcome. I feel so foolish to come here with something so private. But Lucy said this was the perfect place."

Rowtina looked at Lucy, who had her hands on her hips and her mouth open.

"I am sure some of you know men who cheat compulsively." Mercedes continued. "It's a disease, like alcoholism or gambling."

"I'd be kinda happy if George found some other woman who thought she could put up with him," Aggie sighed wistfully.

Mercedes ignored her. "I have made many sacrifices only to be humiliated by the same man again and again." On the last "again," Mercedes looked at Rowtina with an intensity that so unnerved her, Rowtina shifted in her seat, folded her arms, then unfolded them again. Mercedes never mentioned the name of the man who consistently abused her loyalty, but Rowtina pictured his face as vividly as if he'd been in the room with them.

"I know I sound like a child who whines because she cannot

have her way, but I feel so lost, so abandoned, maybe I am a child . . . I cannot tell you how it hurts me."

With an anguished sigh, Mercedes appeared to crumple like a tissue paper doll. There were folds and wrinkles in her blouse and pants, which only minutes before seemed to sculpt her like a second skin. The only part of her appearance that seemed to be unaffected by this collapse was her hair, which tumbled dramatically forward yet remained full as a hot air balloon.

One could only imagine the torment in her face, because you couldn't see it at all. When Mercedes did finally lift her head, her eyes gazed bravely toward the ceiling. It was as though she'd emerged from the deep waters of her grief, shaken yet dry-eyed and miraculously glamorous.

The moment was so astounding, so breathtaking, that Rowtina could tell the Sisterhood was waiting for a moment to be sure it was over. Mercedes held her pose, slightly bent forward in pain, head toward heaven, hair cascading brilliantly down her back. Osceola reached for Mercedes's hand. Mercedes seemed startled by the gesture for a moment. Finally she exclaimed, "Thank you, thank you, may God bless you!" and took Osceola's hand very briefly before dropping it.

Rowtina was glad she'd filled Nelda and Osceola in on Mercedes a bit, so that they might have some perspective on this exhibition.

"Is there anything else you want to say?" Osceola asked Mercedes. "We don't offer any solutions. We're not marriage counselors. But we want you to know we'll be here for you to listen and offer what we can."

Mercedes looked puzzled. "You mean I tell you something like this and that's it?"

"Well, we can't stop him from doing what he does. We're here for you. What is it you want to do?"

Mercedes looked directly at Rowtina, then back to Osceola.

"I want to cut off his balls," she laughed. "And use the same knife on the woman."

Aggie whistled. "Damn!"

Osceola smiled and told Mercedes, "I think we all know that feeling. But short of that, we'll try to think of something. Won't we?" She turned to the other women. Rowtina made herself look at Mercedes, but Mercedes had wrapped herself around Osceola.

"I see why Lucy says what she does about you. You're a good woman." She faced the rest of the women. "But please forgive me if I don't stay for the rest of the meeting. I have lots of important clients this afternoon. I thank you again for all of your kindnesses."

Mercedes turned and clickety-clacked her way back through the chapel doors.

"Well, I'll be damned," Lucy said. "I want you all to know that no matter what that broad just said, I had no idea she was coming. I only went to that shop because I wanted to get an appointment with that Picasso guy. She told me he was all booked up, but I could have her instead."

"She's crazy out of her mind, that's for sure." Aggie shook her head.

Lucy went on. "When she saw that I knew you, Rowtina, she asked me a thousand questions about you. I told her I didn't know you all that well, but that we were in the same Sisterhood and that's how I got to meet you the first time. She was curious about the Sisterhood and naturally I wanted to make her feel welcome. So I told her where we met and what time. And she says that it's really beautiful about the Sisterhood and all, but she has cramps all of a sudden and can't do my hair. Do you believe it?"

Rowtina turned to Nelda. "You don't remember me telling you two about that woman?"

"So she's the hairdresser's partner," Nelda said, putting it together.

"I'm afraid so," Rowtina sighed.

"And the man she was talking about is the same man you've been so obsessed with, this Picasso character?" Osceola stared.

"Obsessed with?" Lucy was stunned.

"Aggie is right. She is crazy, Rowtina, and desperate." Osceola looked toward the chapel door.

"But you're not still seeing him, are you?" Nelda asked. "I thought we'd already taken care of this. Whatever happened to the Higher Plane?"

"What the hell's a higher plane?!" Lucy looked at all of them, realizing how much about any of this she didn't know. "She didn't say anything to me about you and Picasso. She didn't even speak to you just now."

"You don't get that's the point?" Aggie asked her. "She was makin' it plain without callin' Rowtina's name. She ain't playin' with her. She said it. She's ready to do some cuttin.'"

"Well, I'm not afraid of her," Rowtina said. But she didn't know why she wasn't. She remembered Harry Belafonte telling Dorothy-Carmen he'd kill her himself rather than lose her to another man. "Do it then," she'd told him. "Kill me now and be done with it." When Rowtina had first seen Harry carry out his threat, it had frightened her. Now she felt more like Dorothy-Carmen. Mercedes didn't scare her. She'd probably meant every word she'd said, but Rowtina wasn't about to run anywhere.

Osceola stood directly in front of her. "Now, you claim you're not in love, so it ought to be very simple. Tell him you're not interested. If you're lonely, pray to God to send you somebody else. But don't be foolish. You understand?"

Rowtina looked at Osceola as she'd looked at her own mother many times before. It was the same look as when she was thirty-two and Sylvia Mention stood in front of her and said, "You've got to promise me you won't even consider marrying a man who's decided it's perfectly alright to be a delivery boy for the rest of his life." Sylvia Mention reminded her that in situations like these, decent women didn't argue with mothers who'd sacrificed everything to feed and clothe them. Decent women lowered their heads and said, "I don't know what's come over me. I really don't." And because Sylvia Mention taught her daughter that decent was also righteous, decent was reasonable, godly, and good, Rowtina gave Osceola, who was old enough to be her mother, a decent response. She answered her in a voice that was at once both affectionate and respectful. She lowered her head and said what was expected of her. "You're right. I'm not in love. How could I be? It hasn't been a year since my husband died. I don't know what came over me, I really don't."

As soon as she said it, something gurgled and bubbled in her—the sound of Dorothy-Carmen's mocking laughter in the distance. Without thinking, Rowtina checked to see if her seams were straight.

Twenty

Rowtina was sorry she'd made promises she knew she wouldn't be keeping. She didn't want to lie to Osceola anymore than she'd wanted to lie to her mother, but it didn't feel like she had any choice.

There were Spanish markets in the neighborhood, but she decided that putting together a menu of food she wasn't familiar with was much too risky. Instead, Rowtina came up with the idea of going to Estrada's, a tiny Mexican restaurant across from Mount Olive. She'd gone there a couple of times with Nelda and stopped in occasionally for takeout after her shift. The owner made a point of introducing himself and always seemed to remember her.

Rowtina took it as a sign of good luck that before she could ask for him, he appeared from the kitchen in his crisp white shirt, pants, and apron. "Hola!"

"Hola, Andres!" she called to him. "I came to ask your advice. I want to cook a Mexican dinner."

"For yourself?"

"For myself and a friend."

Andres continued to smile and nod yes gallantly. "Do you want something fancy? I can make something especially for you and have it delivered, if you like."

"No, thank you, I want to cook it myself. I thought maybe you could give me a recipe."

"But because this is your first time, it would have to be some-thing simple. I could do something not so simple, but delicious. And for a very good price."

"Maybe I can buy a recipe book on the corner." Rowtina was annoyed with Andres's insistence on catering her dinner. "Sorry to have disturbed you, Andres." She turned to leave, trying not to look disappointed.

"I'm sorry to have offended you," Andres called to stop her. "I can tell you about a very simple dish. Only black beans, pinto beans, rice, peppers, cheese, guacamole, and chorizo."

"Chorizo?" Rowtina asked.

"Sausage. Very spicy. Lots of garlic."

With a twinge, Rowtina remembered she and Turtle had agreed to give up pork the first year they were married. Turtle had made his case to her: "How you gonna call somebody a pig like it's the lowest creature in the world and then sit down to the table and eat some?"

Rowtina wasn't sure she'd be preparing any pork for Picasso's dinner, much less pork with lots of garlic. But she was getting the advice she'd asked for from an expert, so she took note of each ingredient with nods of appreciation.

"Now the secret to making it really Mexican," Andres told her, "is jalapeños! You want your evening a little hot? You let your guest know." He grinned a little more suggestively than Rowtina felt comfortable with.

"How many peppers," she asked, "do you suggest?"

"It is up to the cook," he said, "how much fire she wants to serve."

In the *groceria* at Fourteenth Street and Ninth Avenue, Rowtina bought all of the ingredients Andres had dictated, with the exception of the pinto beans. *Even if that is the way they*

*make it in Mexico, I've got to use my own judgment. And getting
to know somebody better over a plate full of two kinds of beans is
definitely not my idea of a party mixer.*

She remembered what Andres had said about the jalapeños.
She grabbed a handful, declaring her shopping finished. *I don't
know if I'm trying to do what Andres thinks I'm trying to do, but I
don't want anything to be missing, either. Other than the pinto
beans.* Before Rowtina got to the counter with her basket, though,
she turned back to the peppers and got another quarter pound.

Stopping off at the Casa del Musica, Rowtina bought a cas-
sette tape of Luis Miguel. She probably wouldn't know what he
was singing, but she thought Picasso would be impressed that
she owned a tape of Spanish music.

Her last stop was the liquor store, which was helpful enough
to have all of its wines efficiently categorized by country of ori-
gin. Although Rowtina was inclined to choose from the basket of
one-of-a-kind specials, she decided, *I can't scrimp on the wine.*
She remembered watching the cook on television with the pen-
ciled-in eyebrows remind his audience, "Remember, my
cherubs! Fine dining begins with fine wine-ing!" Rowtina paid
eleven dollars for a Spanish rosé called Queen Isabella.

She lit candles and placed them around her bathtub. June's
Essence magazine said bathing by candlelight calmed the senses
that needed calming and aroused those that could use some
encouragement.

Sinking into the warm water, Rowtina closed her eyes and
began to massage her temples like it said to do in the article.
There was the unmistakable presence of someone standing near.
Of course! It makes perfect sense that you would come now.

Rowtina stood and pulled her towel off the rack, wrapping it
around herself. She put on her robe and belted it tightly.

"Turtle, now you listen to me. You haven't been anywhere around for weeks. Don't tell me you don't know how miserable I was. I stopped sleeping so I could be awake whenever you decided to drop by. But I'm almost back to sleeping through the night. And I intend to keep sleeping."

Rowtina strode from the bathroom to the kitchen, not sure if Turtle was following, but as long as she was pretty sure he was finally there, she had to tell him this.

"I've got to stop myself from waiting for you, Turtle. It's not right, if you won't do your part."

She went into the bedroom, breathing as hard as if she'd run five miles with ten pound weights on her wrists and ankles. "That's all I have to say. I know you probably expect more, but that's all I have to say."

Rowtina stood, suddenly releasing her arms so they fell to her sides. Her robe fell open and her towel began to slip. Pulling it from her, she dropped it onto the floor. She removed her robe and stood naked in the center of her bedroom. She announced, "I'm going to get dressed now. I suppose you know I'm having . . ."—and this was the first time she faltered—"company." Rowtina proceeded to her dresser with one hand on her hip, the other flat against her breasts. Her chin cut the air ahead of her in defiance.

She was mixing a few more chopped jalapeños into the salsa when the buzzer rang. Rowtina threw the last few bits into her mouth. Her tongue felt like she'd put it over an open flame. *What did I do that for?*

Picasso had a box of chocolates in one hand, a bottle of wine in the other.

"Hola!" she greeted him, although it sounded ludicrous to her the moment she'd said it. He was wearing a white linen shirt that made him look browner than she'd remembered and a pair of doe-colored cotton jeans that, as usual with Picasso, suggested what you were seeing was his doe-colored butt.

"A little wine, a little chocolate." Picasso presented both to her. She backed away from him into the kitchen, murmuring "Gracias," and made a promise to herself. *That's it. No more bad Spanish. Stop before the man asks you to.*

She called from the kitchen, "I already have some rosé chilled. Unless you'd prefer what you brought."

"Chilled rosé, by all means."

Rowtina came out with their glasses, proudly. "It's Queen Isabella."

"I beg your pardon?"

"The wine," she answered. "It's Queen Isabella." He smiled at her kindly, although he didn't seem to recognize Queen Isabella at all. Eventually, he turned to the bookcase and stared at Turtle's framed photograph.

"That's my husband."

"Turtle."

"That's right."

"And did you love him very much?"

Rowtina answered Picasso and told Turtle again as well, in case he was listening. "Yes. I love him very much."

She sat on the couch. "Now you must tell me about Mercedes."

Picasso turned away from Turtle toward Rowtina. "There is little to tell, actually. What I can say is that she's not my wife or my lover, either. Is that enough?"

"But you must have seen that she acts as though you are. Why is that?"

"Time, maybe. We grew up together, begging side by side for change from Americans at the Tijuana border." Picasso strolled toward Rowtina and sat at the other end of her small couch.

"Our mothers brought us to the customs' ramp every morning at the same time and we competed with each other. She was tougher than I was. I had a crush on her by the time I was twelve. She'd chase a six foot man right onto the highway if she thought he'd give her a dollar. And when he did, she'd run it over to her mother and be back on the ramp demanding more tourista cash in about thirty seconds.

"Somehow, she finally realized I was a boy, not only her competition. We started to both lose money flirting with each other. By that time, we were also both ashamed of begging." Picasso smiled. Sadly, Rowtina thought.

"Our mothers didn't think they had choices. Too many babies, not enough food, and no jobs. But Mercedes and I both knew we hated the way the Americans looked at us before they tossed their nickels. We decided we'd come together to "the New York City"—that's what we called it—and make them want to give us their money. Lots of it."

"And did you? Come here together?"

"No. I came first, by way of L.A. I was the middle boy. My parents weren't afraid for me to leave. They kissed me and told me, 'Do good for yourself.' That was it. Mercedes had a harder time getting out. It's different sending a girl out to beg, especially a girl as beautiful as Mercedes. No matter how tough she thinks she is. Mercedes's mother was . . . greedy. She asked more than she had a right to, especially as Mercedes got older. By the time she got away from her mother and that ramp, I think Mercedes would have walked here barefoot if there wasn't any other way."

It wasn't difficult for Rowtina to picture Mercedes as a relentless, willful child. But the image of the two of them begging to feed themselves was harder.

"What happened to your crushes on each other?"

"I was sixteen when I left home. Even then, I no longer felt the same way. I loved her like a sister, though, and I would have taken her with me if I could have. When she finally got here, it was definitely my family coming to be with me, not a lover."

"But"—Rowtina tried to tread as delicately as she could—"I don't think she thinks of herself as 'Picasso's kid sister.'"

Picasso laughed and sank further into Rowtina's couch, legs spread wide as he faced her.

"Mercedes knows how I feel. She knew before she got here. She's protective of me, that's all. She's my little Sister Bear."

"Mmm. Sister Bear seems about right." Rowtina decided not to press it any further.

Picasso held his glass toward her. "Your Queen Isabella is very good." He surveyed her table. "It's a shame we won't be eating by candlelight."

Immediately, Rowtina pulled two fourteen inch tapers out of the cupboard. Picasso laughed as they sat down across from each other at her tiny table. He tasted Rowtina's cooking.

"So on top of being beautiful and smart, you can prepare an excellent Mexican meal with only days' notice."

Rowtina glowed. "You think it's alright?"

"Much more than alright. Wonderful."

"Not too spicy?"

Picasso laughed. "You obviously have a taste for jalapeños."

He reached across the table with a slice and tucked it between her lips. She surprised herself, catching his finger between her teeth and holding it there, gently.

Luis Miguel began to sing about his Spanish guitar. Picasso reached across the table and pulled Rowtina up to dance. When she put her arm around him, she felt his spine and the meat of his back on either side. He held on to her, clasping above her hips, then turned her swiftly so that she had to lean back against his chest, her hips flush against his thighs. *Oh*

Lord, Luis Miguel is not the only one ready to play his Spanish guitar tonight.

Rowtina stopped dancing. She reached down to the table and took another bit of sliced jalapeño, feeding it to Picasso. "Ahoo," he sang, and took a quick sip of Queen Isabella, offering her some from his glass. Rowtina was feeling bolder by the second. She took several more slices of pepper and slid them into her mouth. Looking up at him, she felt her gypsy earrings graze her neck and she thought, *I am Dorothy Dandridge. You are Harry Belafonte. I want you to blow my toenail polish dry and desert the army for me. Come when I call you. And don't ever keep me waiting.*

It was when she took Picasso's hand and started to lead him into the bedroom that she began to hear the voice. She backed up against the bed to steady herself, to clear her head. Picasso came after her, and she heard it again. She began to shiver. Picasso kissed her shoulders and the shivering got worse, as though he was blowing cold air on her.

She became too dizzy to stand and sat suddenly on the side of the bed. When she looked up and saw the surprise on Picasso's face, she knew he'd misread her. He tried to ease her gently back. She thought she'd have to tell him, "You can't lie here. You can't lie here in Turtle's place, in Turtle's bed."

But Rowtina didn't say anything and the voice got louder. She rolled to the other side, Turtle's side. At least Picasso wouldn't be on Turtle's side.

That's when she felt the tingling. From her hip, to her thigh, all the way down her calf, a tingling. Then the whole leg went numb. She tried to lift it, but she couldn't. As Picasso reached for her, she began to panic.

There was a low sigh. Rowtina looked up at Picasso, but she already knew it hadn't come from him.

She felt as if she were pinned in one spot by a weight heavy enough to crush her completely, yet she felt no pain. Only warmth. Like lying on a beach naked with a high noon sun laying into every crease and fold.

"I've got one foot in love. Lookin' for a sweet leg to lay on."

She might have cried out. Not because she was afraid, or even ashamed, but because Turtle was as real to her as he'd ever been and he'd taught her it was alright to cry out, it was good. But now there was another man standing over her, too, wanting her, and she couldn't tell him why she didn't want him because she'd invited him in. And because they both knew she'd thought she wanted him only moments before.

"What is it, Rowtina? Have you changed your mind?"

Rowtina searched Picasso's face to see what the truth might do. It was obvious he already knew the answer. Still, she nodded and told him, "I really am very sorry." As she said it, the weight lifted. Rowtina ran her hand over her leg, searching. There was nothing.

Picasso told her, "It's alright. It is." Then he asked, "Would you mind if I stayed, for maybe a little while?"

"If we go back out, into the other room," she said as she sat up slowly.

He took her by the hand and helped her off the bed. In the living room, he kneeled in the middle of the floor, looking up at her. "Come, let's just be together, then."

She allowed him to lie beside her, stroking her forehead, touching parts of her face with fingers as light as feathers. Soon she began to drift off. She couldn't be sure if Turtle was waiting for her in the bedroom. Maybe he'd only been there long enough to force Picasso out. What Rowtina decided, though, was that she hadn't done anything wrong. She'd try to enjoy Picasso's company. After all, he said he'd show up and he did. That was more than Turtle could be counted on for.

Picasso held her and she slept. It was only when she felt him roll over and begin to slide his foot up her calf that she shifted her position so that he had to remove it. As she did, she thought she heard her apartment door open and shut.

He asked her if he could take her to breakfast. Part of her wanted to accept his invitation, because no one had ever asked her before, certainly not a man. She laughed at what her mother would think about her going to breakfast with someone who'd slept with her on the floor and now wanted to jump up and go into a public place without brushing his teeth.

"No thank you. I've got a lot to do around here," she told him.

"On Sunday morning? Nobody works on Sunday morning. I don't. Why should you?"

Rowtina thought again of Sylvia Mention. Her mother thought it bad enough Turtle never set foot in church. But at least Rowtina went fairly regularly. And now? What would she do with this particular Sunday morning? Daydream about her Saturday night?

"I always use mornings to catch up with . . . things before I have to go in."

"But we could spend our morning off together. You could catch up with . . . things next Sunday."

Rowtina went to the door and turned back to him, smiling. "I'm sorry."

Picasso followed her, running his hand over his hair and the stubble on his cheeks and chin. With the same hand, he stroked her face and smiled. "I want to see you again. Will you let me?"

Rowtina opened the door, trying to think of what to answer. She wished she was clever like Nelda. But because she didn't think she was clever at all, she reached for his hand as though he was someone she'd just met. "Yes," she said, shaking it vigorously, "we'll see each other again."

He leaned in to kiss her and she let him, but pulled back quickly. He wouldn't let go of her hand, bringing it up to his unshaven face. He pulled it slowly across his closed eyes, his nose, his prickly cheeks, and finally his lips. "I'm not going to let you get away, Rowtina," he told her.

She kept hearing it as she closed her door and locked it, listening to him walk down her hallway. Rowtina thought of how Harry Belafonte told Dorothy-Carmen, "I'll see you dead before I see you with another man."

She leaned back against her door and shook her head. *You ought to stop going to the movies, Rowtina. You ought to take some kind of vow.*

When the phone rang, she half expected it was him. Instead of her customary "hello," she answered a quick, excited "Yes?"

"I went to sunrise service. I prayed for you, like I usually do. If you're not on your way uptown to your own church, I suppose it means you're not going."

Rowtina began to pace slowly, holding on to the phone. "Good morning, Mama."

"You not feeling well?"

Rowtina answered as simply as she could. "I'm fine, Mama. I feel fine."

"Well, did you find a church down there that you like?"

"No, not yet, Mama. I've got a lot of chores to do. I've got the morning off. There are always so many things to catch up on."

"You ought to plan your time off so you can get to some kind of church, Rowtina. Like my mama told me, Sunday morning you get up and get about God's business. Or the devil will surely find work for you to do instead."

"Yes, Mama, I know." Rowtina looked at the pillows in the middle of the floor that she and Picasso had shared. "Mama, next

Sunday morning, I'll come uptown and we'll go to church together. Okay?"

"That's fine," Sylvia Mention answered. "'Cause even if you don't, I know where I need to be on Sunday morning."

"I'll talk to you a little later," Rowtina said, sighing heavily.

"I'll be here," Sylvia Mention told her, and hung up.

Rowtina looked from the phone back to the pillows in the middle of her living room floor. Then she looked into her bedroom at the bed she hadn't slept in because she hadn't felt she could.

No devil here, Mama. Nobody here but Rowtina.

Twenty-one

Dina rushed in from her break a few minutes after nine that evening, wild-eyed. "Rowtina, something terrible's happened over on Tenth Street! There's so much smoke and sirens, you'd think the whole city was on fire."

Rowtina looked up from the patient on a gurney in front of her. "On Tenth? A fire? Did you see what building?" She tried to think. *There are so many buildings on Tenth, it doesn't have to be his.*

"I couldn't get close enough to actually see it myself. The street's closed off. But people were saying it was a coffee shop and a beauty salon in the middle of the block."

Rowtina scribbled the rest of the form for the patient and handed it blankly to the aide waiting for it. She'd already taken her dinner hour and her break. She had two more hours before she could leave the building again. She let Dina know she shouldn't be disturbed and closed the office door behind her.

"Do you have a listing, please, for Picasso's Salon de Belleza?"

"Picasso's who?"

Rowtina repeated herself, her voice hoarse with fear.

"Is that a business or residence?"

"Business."

"Which borough, please?"

"Manhattan. Tenth Street." *I could've made it over there by now. Please. Please let him be alright.*

Rowtina dialed the number. She felt light-headed, watery-legged. There was no sound at the other end. No ring, no recording saying the phone was disconnected. Only emptiness.

The next two hours were busy and mean. One heart attack, a stab wound, a broken ankle, and a fist fight between two interns. But no news from Tenth Street. When an outside call came in again, Rowtina hoped it would be Picasso. It was Nelda calling down from the sixth floor.

"Hey. You wanna walk home? Maybe we can stop at the Village Inn for a glass of wine."

"I have to go over to Tenth Street, Nelda. Have you heard anything about a fire over there?"

"Are you kidding? We've been at the window all night, watching the street. We saw a whole lotta fire trucks, but no fire. They must have gotten it under control right away. Why? What's that have to do with you getting home?"

"Dina said she was over there on her break. The street's closed off, so she couldn't see for herself either, but people told her it was a beauty salon and a coffee shop that was on fire. In the middle of the block."

"Oh." Rowtina could hear that she didn't have to explain anything else to Nelda. "So we'll go over to Tenth Street, baby girl. Wait for me."

Nearing the corner, Rowtina shuddered. She remembered how months before she'd turned a different corner, to a wall of smoke in Harlem, emergency lights beaming scarlet shafts at the sky. Now she looked for some sign. Missing were the two potted birch trees that framed the entrance to the salon. The middle of the block was a charred disaster, just as 146th Street had been.

Rowtina could also see that the salon was boarded up, but the coffee shop next to it was open for business.

There were no fire trucks, only huge, dark puddles, as though it had rained only on Tenth Street. Rowtina thought, *He's got to be here. If he isn't hurt, he's got to be here.*

Nelda walked a few feet ahead into the coffee shop. Rowtina stood outside for a minute, staring at the salon entrance. The neon sign was smashed. Shards of its bulbs floated on the concrete in muddy pools.

Before Rowtina had time to make up her mind about going into the coffee shop, Nelda was back out, breathless with the news. "They said nobody got hurt."

"Who told you? Are they sure?"

Nelda nodded. "The man at the counter says nobody seems to know how the hell the fire got started because the salon was closed today. But because nobody was in it, nobody got hurt."

Of course the salon was closed. Rowtina knew that already. She'd forgotten. "There's no sign or anything," she said out on Tenth Street, more to herself than to Nelda. "How will people know where to find him?"

"The fire only happened today, Rowtina. The guy probably hasn't had a chance to figure out what he's going to do next."

That reasoning seemed to be enough to allow Rowtina to leave the front of the salon, although she continued to survey the street as they walked. She was certain she'd see Picasso somewhere in the vicinity of his shop. By the time they reached Ninth Street, though, she'd almost given up when they were about to go into their apartment building.

"Rowtiiiiinnnnaaa!"

He looked as though he'd been running for hours.

As she and Nelda waited, Rowtina suddenly got an urge to bolt in the opposite direction. Now that she'd seen Picasso, she knew for certain he was safe. Suddenly, it was all she could do to stand in one place and be there when he got to her.

Picasso ran up, put his hands on her shoulders, then leaned back with an enormous, almost hysterical grin. "So! You'll never guess what happened to me today!"

Before Rowtina could move, much less speak, he looked into her eyes with his hands still firm on her shoulders. "You know, eh?! You've seen it?"

"I have," Rowtina whispered. "Was there much . . . ?"

"What? Damage? I don't know how bad it is. They wouldn't let me go in today. But there's something left. They told me that. They got there too fast for it to be totally destroyed." Picasso turned abruptly to Nelda. "I'm sorry. I didn't mean to be rude."

"Don't be ridiculous," Rowtina told him. "We're the ones who are sorry. We just came from around the corner. Is there anything we can do?"

Picasso looked back at her with a look that made Rowtina embarrassed Nelda was watching. She tried to keep breathing. It seemed to be all she could manage.

"No. It's been a long day for both of us. But I wanted to see you." It didn't seem to matter that he was only speaking to one of them.

Nelda pushed her sunglasses further up onto her hair as a kind of punctuation to the moment. "I guess I've got to get inside. I'm worn out. You gonna be alright, Rowtina?"

"Yes. Yes, I'm fine."

Nelda took one last appraising look at Picasso. She walked slowly to the door as though still deciding if leaving was the best decision. She turned back. "You sure, Rowtina?"

Rowtina let her whole body answer Nelda to reassure her. "I'll talk to you. In the morning."

As Nelda went inside, Picasso apologized to Rowtina. "I don't mean to keep you." He never let go of her, though.

"You can come in, you know." She wanted to be a friend to him. It occurred to her, he'd never told her where he lived. He could have been sleeping on a cot in the back of the salon, for all she knew.

"I want to come in." He moved his fingers down her cheek and tugged gently on her chin. "But I've got to get some rest tonight. Tomorrow we see what we can salvage."

"The man who owns the coffee shop next door told Nelda no one knows how it started."

Picasso put his hands in his pockets and sighed wearily. "No. We don't. Mercedes called me. She was terrified. She tried not to let me hear it in her voice, but I did. I was more concerned that she might be hurt.

"We were closed, but she said she'd gone over to check her book to see if she could cancel somebody's appointment or change it or something. When she got to the shop, the firemen were already knocking out the windows. We don't even know who called them."

At the mention of Mercedes's name, Rowtina backed away. She remembered the last vision she'd had of her, at the Leave Him and Live meeting, weeping dry-eyed over an unidentified man whom she claimed was betraying her.

"Can I see you tomorrow?" Picasso reached for her again.

"I can meet you when I get off work at eleven."

"I'll pick you up at the hospital." He kissed her so quickly that she didn't have time to try to stop it. But she didn't return it.

She was trying to think of a way to tell him she couldn't meet him at the hospital. But Picasso had begun kissing her eyes and her nose. When he moved to her neck, she pulled away.

"I'll see you tomorrow," she practically moaned, and ran for her door. As she turned back to glimpse Picasso one last time, she thought she saw not one, but three shadows between them. One was unmistakably Sylvia Mention's, the second was Turtle's, and the third looked curiously like her own.

Picasso waved, with the passion of a twenty year old soldier going off to save his country, but Rowtina was too stunned to see him. She'd already turned from him again and bolted toward safety.

She sat in her living room, carefully avoiding the photograph of Turtle. She wanted to think of exactly what to say, knowing how important it was for her to be honest, forthright. No matter what mistakes she might have made, she knew she must sound strong, unafraid.

When she was reasonably sure of herself (which meant she was not at all sure, but felt she must get on with it anyway), Rowtina approached the bookcase. She picked up the photograph of Turtle, remembering that the last person to handle it had been Picasso Alegria.

Rowtina studied Turtle in his UPS uniform, standing next to his truck. He looked solemn, formal, both of which were unusual for him. It was as though he wanted whoever looked back at him to know a side of him he rarely showed. It was one of the reasons Rowtina had originally not been sure she liked the picture. The man in it looked too close to the Turtle she'd only seen when he was troubled, or angry. But it seemed the picture had won out. Rowtina placed it on the bookcase one day in the living room, avoiding the bedroom, but agreeing to live with it, no matter how somberly Turtle stared back at her.

"Turtle, we have to come to some kind of understanding. Now, I don't believe that you would hurt me or anybody else. I only know a man has come very close to losing everything he's worked for and I pray you didn't have anything to do with it. If I've hurt you, I'm truly sorry. But if it means anything at all, I'm not sure myself why I've done some of the things I've done. It doesn't even feel like me doing them. But this man who depends on his shop to make a living hasn't caused you any harm, Turtle. So I ask you, if you had anything at all to do with that fire, and forgive me if you didn't—but if you did, please don't do anything else to hurt Picasso Alegria."

When she was finished, Rowtina turned off the lights and went into the bedroom. She listened for Turtle. Once she was in bed, she watched for him, or at least signs that he was near. But there was nothing.

Hours later, she awoke with the sensation that someone was sitting at her bedside. She prepared herself before opening her eyes, remembering her promise to herself to appear unafraid, no matter what she faced.

As it turned out, it was not Turtle at all who was sitting at Rowtina's bedside. It was Dorothy-Carmen. And she wasn't alone. Standing next to her was Pearl-Frankie, who was really a combination of Pearl Bailey, Osceola McQueen, and Nelda Battey.

It might have been easier not to seem afraid if it had been Turtle who'd appeared to her. At least she'd half expected Turtle. Rowtina couldn't bring herself to say anything to these women.

Dorothy-Carmen began with a low hum. It felt to Rowtina as though the floor began to vibrate with the sound of her voice. The tune was eerily familiar to Rowtina. Whether it was the melody or the sound of Dorothy-Carmen's voice, she wasn't sure, but Rowtina suddenly felt cold to the bone. Chilled as if it had been the dead of winter with no heat in the apartment and she'd been sleeping naked without even a sheet to warm her.

Pearl-Frankie began also, in what Rowtina heard as two voices, in two different octaves. She'd never heard either of them sing before, but it was Nelda and Osceola, Rowtina knew for sure, somewhere inside the vision standing over her.

They began to spit out the words in a metallic three-part harmony, and Rowtina, thinking it was not possible, got colder. She knew the song. It was what Dorothy-Carmen had sung when Pearl-Frankie cut her deck of cards and turned up the nine of spades, the Death card.

"It ain't no use to run away from dat 'ol boy if he is chasing you."

Rowtina might have leapt out of bed if she'd had the courage. She might have ordered them—however many there were—to leave her bedside immediately and go try to intimidate somebody else. But she had the ability neither to form words nor move from her place in the bed. She had no choice but to wait, immobile, barely breathing, until they'd finished.

She didn't remember them leaving. But she knew better, in the morning, than to fool herself into thinking it was merely a dream. *They were here, alright. Even if I'm the only witness, I know they were here.*

She knew she couldn't tell anyone. Barring that, there wasn't actually very much she could do. Except wait. And as Sylvia Mention always admonished her, "Pay attention. Pay good attention."

Twenty-two

"Hey. Taking a dinner break?"

"Oh, Nelda. It's you."

"Sorry to disappoint you, darlin', but yeah, it's me. I repeat, Ms. Rowtina, ma'am, are you taking a dinner break or do you have a better offer?"

"No. No, I'm not taking a break tonight. I was thinking I'd stay down here."

"Are you that busy?"

"No . . ."

"Then take a dinner break. You can keep me company."

"Alright. I guess so. I'll meet you in the cafeteria."

Rowtina gave Dina explicit instructions. "If anyone calls, please tell them I'll be gone no longer than a half hour. Please take a message. And make sure you get their number."

She hadn't wanted to leave her desk at all until it was time to sign out at the end of the night. She wanted to be there if Picasso called. Instead, she met Nelda. Rowtina tried to look relaxed, but made it clear to Nelda from the beginning that she couldn't stay for very long.

"I'm expecting a call," she told her, looking distractedly around the room.

"I see," answered Nelda, with a half-smile. "Well, you tell me when you have to leave, then. I'm only here to help. You don't have to explain anything."

Rowtina fidgeted silently as Nelda inhaled a pot roast sandwich, two cupcakes, and a large chocolate milk. Finally Nelda told her, "You win. You are the lousiest damn dinner company I've had in a very long time. The next time you tell me you don't want to take a dinner break, I will leave your jittery ass alone. Please go back to the emergency room."

"I'm really sorry, Nelda."

"No apology necessary. You warned me, I'm hardheaded, that's all."

By the time Rowtina took the elevator back downstairs to the emergency room, Picasso had called not once, but twice.

"What a sexy voice!" Dina gushed. "He said he was hoping he could speak to you. He didn't want to leave a message."

"Did he give you a number where I could call him back?"

"No, he said he couldn't. He said he was outside the salon, because the phone inside was disconnected." Dina was reading the notes she'd dutifully made during her conversation. "He won't be able to pick you up, but he'll meet you there for sure. Oh"—and for this Dina tried to approximate a seductive, sensuous tone—"he said he's sorry about the change in plans. But he'll make it up to you when you see each other."

Rowtina was at the time clock ready to punch out when Picasso called again. She ran back behind the desk to grab the phone.

"Hello—er—Mount Olive Emergency."

"I was hoping I would be able to catch you. I'm sorry I have to change things."

"It's fine. Is everything alright?"

"Yes, yes, everything is—well, I can't say 'alright.' But it's not bad, now that I'm speaking to you."

Rowtina looked up to see who might be listening, as though they could hear Picasso at the other end. Dina was waving good night and making kissing faces like a twelve year old schoolgirl. Tonya and Emma, the women beginning the next shift, were catching up on hospital gossip, oblivious to Rowtina and her phone conversation.

"I wanted to tell you I may not be here when you come," Picasso told her. "I got a call they want to speak to me at the police precinct about the fire. If you wait for me, I know I won't be long."

Rowtina told him, "If tonight isn't good for you, I understand. I'll go on home."

"Please don't. I want to see you. Come to the shop. I'll tell them I have someone waiting. Say you'll be there."

"Alright. I'm leaving now and I'll wait."

As soon as she hung up, the phone rang again. Having already received the call she'd been waiting for, Rowtina hurried away, leaving Emma or Tonya to answer it. She was bolting through the door when she heard, "Rowtina! Rowtina, it's for you."

She turned, practically snatching the phone from Emma. "Yes. What is it?"

"I was calling to see if you wanted to walk home together. Why the hell are you answering the phone like you got a tick up your ass?"

Rowtina laughed. There were days she and Nelda went without seeing each other at all. Tonight, when Rowtina was again full of secrets, Nelda was demanding answers as if they were longtime lovers. It suddenly occurred to Rowtina, she didn't have to lie. She didn't want to. Nelda, of everyone she knew, should understand not obeying the rules.

"I'm not going home, Nelda. I'm going to meet Picasso."

There was a half second of silence on the other end before Nelda laughed. "I knew that. Yes, I did. I knew that."

"We can walk home together tomorrow night, though."

"Maybe. I'll check my book and let you know. Bye, girl."

Rowtina rushed past Eleventh Street. She studied her makeup and hair in a flower shop window's reflection on the corner. *I'm not sure I like this leopard print scarf I've got tied around my neck. Maybe I went too far.* Dorothy-Carmen, she remembered, wore scarves around her neck. Would she have worn a leopard print? Rowtina had thought a scarf might make her look a little more sophisticated tonight. And Sylvia Mention wouldn't ever know that her daughter was wearing an inexpensive leopard print scarf tied around her neck. So she couldn't possibly be embarrassed by her.

At Tenth Street, she realized she'd forgotten that the potted trees she'd admired on either side of the salon door were not there anymore. Not only were the trees missing, but there was now a flat, empty darkness where the dreamlike neon blue had only days ago spelled out the owner's name. As she approached the shop, the business she knew Picasso had worked years for looked abandoned, desolate.

Rowtina thought she'd have seen him by now. He said he'd try not to keep her waiting. She hadn't really stopped to think what the police wanted to see him about in the first place. What did they think had actually happened to Picasso's salon?

She'd go into the coffee shop next door until he came. *I'll get a table next to the window. That way I'll be sure to see him when he comes.*

There was a sizable late-night crowd inside and no tables were available, so Rowtina went directly to the counter.

"Hi there. What can I do for you, ma'am?" The counterman slid a napkin, fork, knife, and spoon in front of her.

"I was actually waiting for someone. The owner of the salon next door. You haven't seen him, have you?"

"Picasso? Yeah, he was in here a couple of hours ago. He got a coffee to go and went right back in the shop. Poor guy, I think he's trying to do some kind of inventory in there. Figure out exactly how bad the damage is. 'Scuse me." He moved down the counter to a couple waiting for change.

It was just enough news about Picasso to make Rowtina more anxious, but there was still no sign of him and she thought she might ask the counterman one more question. Eventually, when the couple had their change and paid their bill, he came back down to her end.

"So, did you want to order something while you wait? Cup of coffee?"

"I'm not sure. Did you say you haven't seen him since he came in before? And that was hours ago?"

"A couple hours, yeah. But then we've been pretty busy. He could have come and gone a few times by now. Did you knock on the door? You can't really tell who's in there with everything boarded up like that."

The counterman had made Rowtina's mind up for her. "No. I didn't knock. I guess that's what I'll do. Thanks." She eased off the stool feeling a little guilty at not having ordered anything. "Thank you very much. I really appreciate it."

Between the plywood boards covering the door, she could see a light coming from the back of the shop. So he was there already. She hadn't needed to go into the coffee shop at all. She should have known he was there.

Rowtina knocked lightly on the boarded up door that she'd first seen as tinted pale blue glass with a scroll design etched around the border. She waited a moment and knocked again a little harder. She didn't want to call out. Besides, he was expecting her. It would only be a moment before he realized what time it was and came to the front. Or maybe he was playing music and couldn't hear her knock. She went from the door to what had been a huge glass window, now a plywood mass already scarred by graffiti. "The Magician Was Here" was scrawled inside what was supposed to be a cape but looked more like a giant mushroom or an umbrella.

Rowtina knocked on the wood-covered window. She was becoming self-conscious about being seen trying to get into this boarded up shop. *Maybe I should just wait. I'll give him another couple of minutes and then I'll go home. He can call me there. If he wants to see me.*

She went to the door and glanced once more at the light in the back of the salon. Then she turned and tried to look like it was not at all suspicious for a black woman to be standing alone in front of a burned-out building in Greenwich Village. The woman in the gypsy earrings with the whiskey voice who wasn't afraid to be seen anywhere didn't seem to be around tonight.

After about a minute and a half, Rowtina peered between the plywood cracks, telling herself this was the very last time. *Then I'm definitely going home.*

There was still no sign of anyone inside. Rowtina took a deep breath, looked in both directions, and tried to turn the doorknob. To her surprise, the door was unlocked. It swung open noiselessly. Rowtina stepped inside quickly and shut it behind her.

"Picasso! It's Rowtina. Are you here?"

He didn't answer. The room was dim and shadowy, but there was no mistaking the damage that had been done. From the slivers of light between the boards on the door, Rowtina could see that the front room had been gutted, except for a waterlogged carpet covering the floor. She also realized the light was coming from the back of the salon.

There was also sound. Rowtina couldn't hear what it was at first, but as it got louder, she knew, of course, it was music. Spanish music. A woman singing low like a saxophone. Then a shout. A throbbing of horns.

"Picasso!" Rowtina smiled. The uneasiness that had begun to overtake her, the gnawing panic, began to subside. Picasso was waiting for her.

She walked swiftly toward the light, carefully dodging the murky pools of water on the soggy carpet. There was a room she hadn't noticed when she was there as a customer. It was further back than where she'd been. The door was partially open. Rowtina called over the music, "Picasso?" She knocked on the door and waited. When there was still no answer, she pushed it open gently.

A huge desk sitting in the middle of rubble from the ceiling and a filing cabinet in the corner seemed to be all that was left of an office. Rowtina stepped inside.

"Picasso went to get something. Probably for your date tonight. I decided I would keep you company until he returned."

In a pair of dark pants and shirt, her feet wide apart in what looked like men's oxfords, stood Mercedes. Her hair was pulled back and, as far as Rowtina could tell, she was wearing no makeup. She looked like the young girl Picasso had described growing up with, complete with a look of steely determination and contempt. She was holding a half empty water glass of what appeared to be liquor.

"I can wait outside. I don't mind." Rowtina didn't know where Picasso was, and for the moment, she didn't care. Whether he knew Mercedes would be there when she arrived Rowtina also didn't know, but what was most important was that she get out.

"I would say welcome. But we both know how insincere it would be. You already know you were never welcome here. You're an intruder. Who else would come into a boarded up building that was obviously closed but an intruder?"

"I'll go. I said I'd wait outside." Rowtina tried to sound as firm and determined as Mercedes did. She tried to make her body move toward the door. Mercedes wasn't in front of it. Rowtina wanted to walk right out of the office, out of the shop, and into the street. But her body refused to help her. It waited as though it knew the only way to leave was if permission was granted.

"It's too late. You're already inside," Mercedes hissed at her sharply. "Picasso said he didn't think you'd try to come in. But I knew better. If I didn't know so well who you are, you might have surprised me, coming back here through the dark. I could easily have thought you'd broken in to see what was left."

"But I didn't break in. The door was open and I—"

"And you walked right in without anyone asking you to. Isn't that what thieves do? I don't really know that you haven't come to try to steal something, do I? Maybe I should try to protect myself."

Mercedes still wasn't blocking the door. Rowtina decided if she only thought that she could walk out and keep walking, then she could.

Slowly, Mercedes began to grin. "I am only making a joke with you. You should see how frightened you look." She took a quick sip from her glass and did a dance step to the music as though she'd been snatched into another world. She stopped as abruptly as she'd begun.

"Yes, he loves me. I know that he does. And when intruders come, it only takes a little while before they know that he is already taken. He cannot be stolen. Something tragic always happens when they try to steal him. You see? All that we've worked for together. Ruined. That's what happens when thieves come sneaking in, trying to take what does not belong to them."

Rowtina searched the room. For what, she wasn't sure. Maybe she expected one of the walls might fall away like a movie set and leave the shop exposed to the street. Maybe Picasso was standing in a corner she'd overlooked and now he'd step forward and ask Mercedes very quietly to stop talking madness. He'd apologize to Rowtina and she'd tell him it was fine, it was alright, she was simply relieved he'd been there, hiding in the corner.

"I'm sorry you think I'm intruding. But Picasso and I hardly know each other."

"You're not one year a widow, they tell me. Yet you sleep with men you say you hardly know." Mercedes leaned forward toward Rowtina, daring her to refute it. "Either you had a very bad marriage, or you have found a way of mourning your husband that is both selfish and dangerous."

Rowtina stumbled backward as if she'd been punched. "I want to leave now. Will you please let me leave?"

"You are a damned coward, Mrs. Rowtina Washington. *Una cobarde,*" Mercedes shot at her. "Why don't you walk out if you want to leave instead of begging for permission? No one asked you to come in, remember? Remember?!"

There was a muffled *pop.* Rowtina jumped. At the same time, she saw blood spurt from Mercedes's hand. Mercedes dropped what was left of the glass as though it had bitten her. There was still one thick jagged sliver piercing her palm. She groaned, with a look of faint surprise in her eyes. Then, just as quickly, the surprise was gone and the familiar stoniness set in again. Mercedes slowly raised her free hand to her palm and snatched the chunk of glass out.

Rowtina heard footsteps coming toward the office.

"Hola!" Picasso was at the door, carrying a huge bouquet of pale lavender orchids. "What are you two both doing here?" he asked, with a nervous grin. Before either of them could answer, he saw Mercedes's blood-covered hand.

"God," he whispered. "What have you done?"

Mercedes gazed at him placidly. "I've had an accident. That's all. I'll be alright."

Picasso stared at Rowtina. She could only manage to tell him, "You should take her to the hospital. She could lose a lot of blood."

At the same time he tossed the orchids onto the desk, he leaned into Rowtina, his face an eggplant crimson. He grabbed her by both arms, shouting, "What the hell happened here?"

Astounded, Rowtina pulled herself away from him, stuttering, "She, she c-cut herself. You should get her to the hospital."

Mercedes allowed Picasso to grasp her elbow gently. Rowtina realized she was still holding the broken glass. She held out her bleeding hand. "I was trying to protect myself. She was so bold, coming into the shop as if she knew no one would be here. You're not going to leave her here, are you? You can't possibly still trust her. Look! Look at what she did to me!"

The music had stopped. Picasso looked from Mercedes to Rowtina. Rowtina couldn't speak. Whatever he believed, she couldn't speak, and she wouldn't be able to tell him anything different.

Picasso held Mercedes close to him. "Shhhh. You are going to be alright. I'm here and you have to listen to me. We have to get someone to take care of this." He stared again at Rowtina, but she couldn't understand what his eyes were saying. She only knew to follow as he led Mercedes through the shadows toward the front door of the salon.

When they got outside the shop, Rowtina said to Picasso's back, "It'll be faster if you walk to the hospital. It'll take too long to get a cab. Wrap something around her hand to stop the bleeding."

As Picasso began to guide her down Tenth Street, Mercedes turned back and smiled at Rowtina. When the two of them had gone a few feet, Picasso turned back as well, but Rowtina still couldn't understand what he was trying to say.

"Go to the emergency room entrance." Rowtina kept speaking as though she had a recorder inside that continued without any instruction from her. She hadn't moved from where she was standing. "It's on Twelfth Street." And the recorder stopped.

Picasso began to run toward the corner with his arm around Mercedes. Rowtina stared at the two of them, their bodies so close together they appeared to be one strange misshapen person, hurrying away from her.

Twenty-three

Rowtina played it all over in her mind, from the time she left Mount Olive's emergency room until the moment she'd told Picasso he should take Mercedes there. First, she considered what the reality had been. Then she imagined all that might have happened had she said or done something the least bit differently. Eventually, the memory of Mercedes's palm clenching the wedge of glass and the echo of Picasso demanding to know "What the hell happened here?" was louder than all the other sounds and images. Rowtina flinched each time Picasso shouted through her memory. By the time she reached home, it was not Picasso's voice she heard at all. It was her own. *What the hell happened here?* And her voice cut as deeply as the wedge of glass in Mercedes's palm.

Stumbling into her darkened apartment, Rowtina could see the flashing light on her phone, signaling a message had been left. She sank into the folds of her couch but knew immediately she didn't want to stay there. She wanted to be in bed, in a tight knot.

Moving through the living room, she felt detached—no, it was more, she was repulsed. Repulsed by all of the furniture, all of the familiar objects she'd brought from Harlem downtown and shared for years before that with Turtle. Some of them were hand-me-downs from Sylvia Mention, who was convinced

Rowtina's marriage to a delivery boy meant she'd never own any nice things again.

I'm going to throw all of it out, Rowtina told herself. *All of it.*

She didn't have the strength to take off her clothes. She used whatever she had left to step out of her shoes, lie across the bed, pull her knees up to her chest. She was more tired than she remembered feeling in a very long time.

I can't open my fists. My fingers are locked. If I can't open my fists, I can't stop the bleeding.

Rowtina could hear her buzzer, interrupting the dream. Slowly, half awake, she opened her fists, ran her fingers across her palms. They were sore, but she wasn't bleeding. She hadn't been cut, she was sure of it now.

The room seemed cooler. Her forehead was no longer clammy. The fever she was certain she had only hours ago had broken. She was safe. Whole. She didn't get up.

The buzzer was insistent. It was Picasso, she knew, refusing to be ignored.

Minutes later it was clear he had no intention of going away. Rowtina's phone rang, stopped, and then the buzzer began again.

She walked slowly to the next room and pressed the intercom button. "Yes?"

"Please. May I speak to you?" It was the same promise in his voice that she always heard, the same notes within notes that had made her greedy for more.

She answered him by pressing the tiny button marked "DOOR," pushing it just long enough to let him in if he moved quickly. Rowtina glanced down at her stocking feet, her wrinkled dress. *It doesn't matter,* she decided. *It's not important. I'm in my house. I can look like I damn well please.*

She opened her door and waited, a series of images flashing

through her mind. Mercedes. Sneering at her, calling her a coward. Mercedes's hand around the glass of liquor. Picasso. Looking surprised and afraid, then screaming at her. The fury in his eyes. Mercedes. Smiling at her as they turned to go to the hospital.

Then Picasso was there, in front of her. "I've come to ask your forgiveness."

Rowtina stood back, further into the room, still holding on to the door. "Come in." Her own voice sounded foreign to her. It wasn't Dorothy-Carmen or the jazz singer with the red curls. Foreign, yes, but at the core it was her voice, really—only there was something different in it, something unexpected. "How is Mercedes?"

"She's going to be alright. They didn't even have to put in stitches. They used what they call a butterfly."

Rowtina smiled at the word "butterfly" and the last image she remembered of Mercedes with so much hate in her eyes.

"It's you I'm worried about," Picasso told her. "I was so surprised seeing the two of you together, and then so much blood. I didn't know what could have happened."

Rowtina studied his face carefully. "And did she tell you?"

"She only said she'd had an accident."

Rowtina waited. When she realized Picasso seemed to accept Mercedes's explanation, she shrugged to let him know she wouldn't be offering one of her own.

"The important thing now, Rowtina, is for you to know how sorry I am that I got so upset. I—"

"You grabbed me and shouted at me. Because you thought I'd hurt her."

"But I care about you." He reached for Rowtina. She backed away, not in fear but with a look that told him he had neither license nor permission. "I know that you know." He began to purr, she thought, like a big beautiful tawny lion. "I know that you can hear it, even now, in my voice."

Rowtina strode slowly over to the bookcase, where Turtle stared back at her from his photograph. "Maybe that's the problem. I hear so many things. From so many people."

"There is only one thing you should hear from me now. That is—I want you, and I want to be able to come here knowing you want me also, without any question or doubt. Do you think that is possible?"

Rowtina looked at him and pictured how bruised her arms were where he'd grabbed her. She remembered him shouting at her and knowing that Mercedes was right, she was an intruder, a stranger who was being punished for trespassing. She took a deep breath. For a moment, she thought she could hear the Women of Jordan singing, and between the verses Turtle was telling her, "Rowtina, you a woman set apart."

Finally she answered Picasso. "No. No, I don't think that it will be possible."

At first there was only silence. Picasso continued to look at her as though he expected her to either clarify or refute what she'd said. When she did neither, he said patiently, "It's because you're upset with me. I've hurt your feelings. But you have to remember how good we felt to each other, sleeping there together." He gestured toward her floor and Rowtina looked down, half expecting to see some remnant of the night they'd spent.

"I remember," she told him. She walked to the door. "But we hardly know each other, and you're already shouting and grabbing. My husband didn't do either. Ever. And we were married for eight years."

Picasso moved in front of the door to prevent her from opening it. "Please, Rowtina. Let me make it up to you."

Rowtina got as close to him as he'd been to her earlier that night, when he'd demanded to know what the hell was going on. Her voice was low and steady, and there were notes in it she knew came from some part of her body she'd never heard before.

"I want you to leave my home now." She reached past him to open the door. "Right now."

Picasso made strange choking noises in his throat. He ran his hand through his mop of kinky onyx curls and over his mouth. "Please call me," he whispered. Then he left.

For a few long, quiet moments, Rowtina stood looking at the closed door. She turned and walked back to the bookcase, where Turtle was staring solemnly at her from his silver frame.

I guess I got scared, Turtle, didn't I? You wouldn't come back when I wanted you to. I got scared there wouldn't be anybody else. But it's going to be alright now, I think. So you go on, Turtle. And rest.

Twenty-four

The "Message Waiting" light was still blinking like a tiny red eye in the corner of the living room. Rowtina sat in the little wooden chair next to the telephone, a chair with lavender hearts painted on it that she'd had since she was eleven. *This chair will be the first to go and I won't miss it.* She pressed the "Playback" button.

"Hey, baby girl, it's me. Call me. Preferably when you're alone."

Rowtina shook her head and dialed Nelda's number.

"Good morning," she said brightly. "How's my upstairs neighbor?"

"If you think I'm checking up on you, you get a gold star. Are you in one piece?"

Rowtina breathed a deep sigh. "I think so. Let me make sure." She glanced down at the two dark welts on the insides of her elbows. The swelling had gone down. "Yep, I am."

"Good. Now I have something to ask you and I don't want you to be upset."

Rowtina laughed. "You couldn't upset me, Nelda. Not today."

"Well, it's about next Saturday."

"What about it?"

"Osceola wants to drive out to Long Island. Kara's buried out there. Osceola and I rent a car and go together every so often. We clean up around the gravestone, leave some flowers. Osceola wants you to come, but I told her I didn't know if you were ready to do something like that yet. Maybe it's too soon."

Rowtina couldn't answer for a moment. She wasn't sure she could go back to a cemetery. She'd told herself she wasn't ever going back to a grave site if she could help it. Yet somehow, Nelda's request didn't seem so horrible.

"I can go," she said. "Of course I'll go."

"Good." Nelda sounded relieved. "I was actually a little surprised when Osceola brought it up. She's never invited anybody to go out there with us before."

"Well, I hope you won't mind if I come, then."

"No," Nelda said quietly. "Osceola says we're gonna keep making the trip until we both agree that the Kara we knew isn't really there at all. Then we can let the workmen worry about the grave, because we'll understand it's only a patch of dirt. I guess I haven't gotten to that point yet."

"Thanks for asking me, Nelda," Rowtina said. "Thanks to both of you."

Halfway out to the Long Island cemetery, it began to rain. Osceola said to Nelda, "If it gets too heavy, we can turn back, you know. I guess I didn't pick such a good day for this."

But Nelda answered, "We're doing fine. I've driven in rain before, darlin'," and they continued in silence. Rowtina, too, was having second thoughts. *Maybe I don't want to do this. I should ask them to stop the car and let me wait outside the cemetery. Nelda was right. It's too soon.* But she didn't say anything. She sat quietly and tried to prepare herself.

"Steel River" seemed like an odd name to Rowtina, but then, who was to say what an appropriate name for a cemetery might be? Nelda pulled up in front of an office and ran inside. She came back a few minutes later with a large umbrella. "They lent it to us," she said as she got back into the car. "We'll drop it off on the way out."

They drove a little further inside the cemetery before Nelda pulled over again. When they got out of the car, Rowtina realized she could actually look past the field of graves and see the water. Rowtina had never considered a cemetery could look anywhere close to beautiful, but there was something about the river beyond the graves that seemed just that, she thought.

Nelda took Osceola's hand as they approached the grave site. Rowtina walked beside them. She began to tremble. She told herself, *I can't be selfish. This is for Osceola.*

Nelda had said they were going to make sure the area around Kara's grave was clean, but the whole cemetery was so well attended, Rowtina couldn't understand what she and Osceola could have been concerned about. They walked a few feet to a simple marker near a very large oak tree—the three of them huddled under the black umbrella. Osceola had a small bouquet of white tulips, which she laid in front of the marker. She stepped back and began to pray, Rowtina thought, but Osceola was only moving her lips without making a sound at first. Then she began the Twenty-third Psalm. Rowtina felt her trembling getting worse. She could hear Reverend Otillie and her mother. She could see Turtle's coffin set over that enormous hole in the ground.

When Osceola got to "Yea, though I walk through the valley of the shadow of death," Rowtina thought, *We're here again—all of us—in the valley of the shadow of death.* She continued with Osceola, "I will fear no evil."

The three women finished saying the psalm. Nelda had her head on Osceola's shoulder, holding on to her like a small child.

Softly, Rowtina asked Osceola, "Were you ever afraid?"

Osceola nodded. "Oh God, yes. Afraid for my daughter and me too. Scared out of my mind for a very long time."

"And what happened?"

Osceola smiled. "I had a dream Kara told me to let go. So I did." She turned to Nelda. "Are you ready?"

Nelda nodded.

Osceola took Rowtina's hand. It was impossible for Nelda to complete the circle because she was holding the umbrella. She laughed, placed it on the ground, and reached for Rowtina.

The three of them stood in the rain with their heads bowed and their eyes closed, as if they were in the meeting room on the seventh floor of Mount Olive. Rowtina pictured the river just beyond the cemetery. *I wish you had a river, Turtle.* But she thought about what Kara had told Osceola in her dream, and she decided Turtle would be fine where he was, even without a river. She squeezed Osceola's hand on one side, Nelda's on the other.

"Let the circle be unbroken," Osceola began, and Nelda and Rowtina joined in. "Till we meet again."

◫ READING GROUP GUIDE

ONE FOOT IN LOVE

1. To what does the title *One Foot In Love* refer? How does the title suggest some of the other themes in the book? How many situations and characters in the novel do you think the title applies to?

2. After Rowtina returns from the hospital morgue she calls her mother only "because there'd be hell to pay if she didn't." What do we learn about the relationship between Sylvia Mention and her daughter from that obligatory phone call? How has that relationship shaped Rowtina's interaction with other people?

3. For the eight years that Rowtina and Turtle were married she kept her distance from other people, even though Turtle encouraged her to be more social. Rowtina seems to have been content with her life revolving around Turtle. Do you think it is possible for someone to be so in love that he or she doesn't need the companionship of anyone else?

4. Why would Rowtina call in sick with the flu rather than tell her coworkers her husband has died?

5. In spite of her initial reluctance Rowtina finds herself responding to the overtures of friendship from Nelda and the other members of the women's group. How does the encouragement and sisterhood Rowtina experiences from membership in such a group differ from her one-on-one friendship

with Nelda? Early in the book Rowtina decides that she's simply not "cut out to be a club-joining woman." How does the Leave Him and Live group compare to the Women's Auxiliary of Harlem and the Marian Anderson Club?

6. The Leave Him and Live Sisterhood is not only multiracial, but the five women differ in age and life experience. What binds these very different women together?

7. Egyptia creates a scene at her engagement party because she is horrified to see Nelda dancing with her female lover. Even though at the next Sisterhood meeting Egyptia apologizes, Rowtina suspects that the rift between the two women can't be healed. Is Rowtina correct? Have you ever had a serious argument with a close friend that threatened the relationship? How was it resolved? Can you be close to someone even if you don't approve of some of the choices he or she makes?

8. Do you think Turtle appears to Rowtina as a ghost, or are her dreams very realistic? Does it matter?

9. "I'm a Harlem girl," is Rowtina's defense when Nelda teases her about her lack of sophistication about Greenwich Village. "I'm a Harlem girl, too, originally. But it never hurts to expand your horizons," Nelda chides her. Talk about the ways in which Rowtina expands her horizons over the course of the novel.

10. As you were reading the novel, were you rooting for the budding romance between Picasso and Rowtina to succeed or did you think it was a bad match? Why? Do you think it is too soon after Turtle's death for Rowtina to be falling for someone new, or does the timing seem right?

11. How do you account for Mercedes's passionate possessiveness? Do you think Picasso is lying about there being nothing sexual between the two of them? Do you think he is sending Mercedes unclear signals? Or do you think she is simply crazy and he has no control over the situation?

12. Many people would describe *One Foot In Love* as a woman's novel because most of the characters are women and it deals primarily with their concerns. Yet the author is a man. What other books have you read recently that were written by a man but in which the point of view was a woman's? Does a novelist have to be of the same race, gender, ethnicity, religion, or sexual orientation as the book's protagonist in order to render that character convincingly?

13. *One Foot In Love* has several lighthearted moments but deals with very serious themes. Do you think the novel is intended to be serious, funny, or a combination of the two?

Discover more reading group guides online and download them for free at <u>www.bookclubreader.com</u>.

Read Bil Wright's
unforgettable debut novel

"A realistic, poignant story [that] grabs you from the beginning,
tugs at your heartstrings and doesn't let go."
—*Philadelphia Tribune*

Sunday You
Learn How to
Box

a novel

BIL WRIGHT

Author of *ONE FOOT IN LOVE*

0-684-85795-2

TOUCHSTONE
A Division of Simon & Schuster
A VIACOM COMPANY

MG

3√
6 4